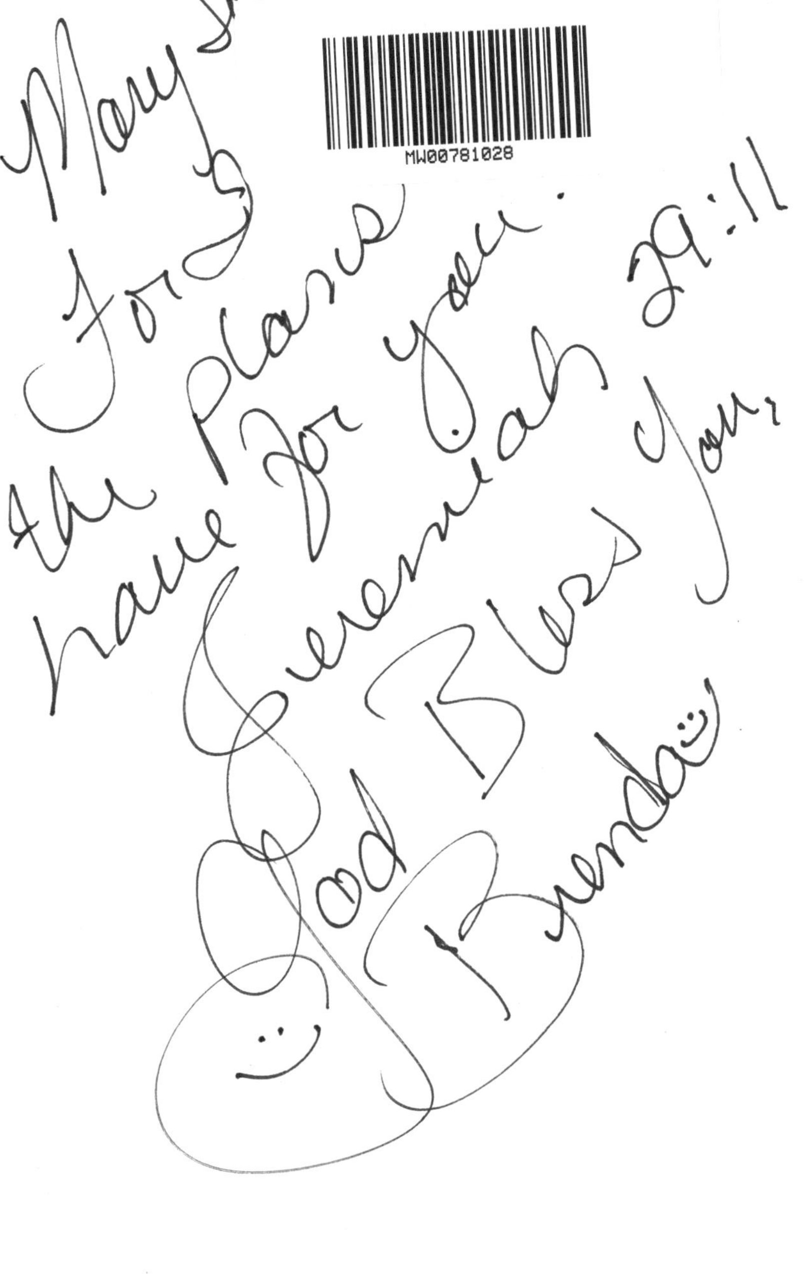

MW00781028

Mary [illegible]

For [illegible]

the plans

have for you.

Jeremiah 29:11

God Bless You,

Brenda :)

:)

ANGEL WING MINISTRIES PRESENTS

. . .

Saving Noelle

CARRIED BY ANGELS SERIES

BOOK NUMBER 1

Brenda Conley
Angel Wing Ministries

Carried By Angels Series…Book 1...SAVING NOELLE.

Please note that I have chosen to capitalize certain pronouns in Scripture that refers to the Father, Son, and Holy Spirit. And I have made a personal choice not to capitalized the word satan. That may differ from some Bible publishers' styles.

A special thank you for the use of the beautiful words to the song "ARMS THAT HOLD THE UNIVERSE" BY FEE.

I would like to acknowledge the use of material from the booklet "WHAT DOES GOD SAY ABOUT ABORTION". Focus On The Family ©2001

Library of Congress Cataloging in-Publication Data

Conley, Brenda

Saving Noelle/Brenda Conley

ISBN-13 978-0615628851 (Angel Wing Ministries)

ISBN-10 0615628850

COVER
DESIGN
CREATED BY

Brandon Andrina

DEDICATION

This book belongs to all the broken women who live everyday with the grief of losing a child to the lies of abortion.

God sees your brokenness. He wants to restore you. Our God is in the restoration business and He loves you.

Do not let satan tell you differently. He wants you to live a lifetime of brokenness. He is a liar who comes to kill, steal and destroy. He will never have a victory unless you give it to him. He has already been defeated. Jesus himself went into hell and took back the keys so that satan could have no control over any area of your life.

There is no sin that is too big for our God to forgive. He does not want you to live a life carrying a load of regret. He made a way through His Son Jesus Christ to lighten that load and give you hope. In fact, He will pick you up and carry you when the road seems to long…when you are too weary… when you have gone as far as you can…when you can see no hope at the end of the day..

If you are still burdened with choices that you made, today is the day to lay them at the feet of Jesus. He is just waiting for you to come just as you are. Broken and spilled out, surrendered to Him. Feel the freedom that only He can give. Run to His mercy seat and live with joy. Jesus is just waiting to change your life. He wants to give you a life everlasting full of love, hope and peace; the peace that surpasses all understanding.

By ourselves we will never be worthy. But through Christ all things are possible. He loves you enough that He laid down His life for you so that you could live a life abundant. You were created with a purpose. God knew that purpose even before you were brought into this world. Seek Him. Find Him. Live for Him.

A SPECIAL ACKNOWLEDGEMENT TO THE GROUP "FEE"

The night that I began this journey with Noelle, I sat down at my computer and turned on my Itunes as I sometimes do when I write. The music softly began to play a new CD that I had recently gotten and not heard yet. It was from a group that I did not know called "Fee". The song was "The Arms That Hold the Universe". As the words played on, I could feel Noelle's heart breaking through the story of the song.

I began to incorporate the words into the first chapter.

"I know it seems like this could be the darkest day you know.

Through the words of the song, the breaking of Noelle's heart became so real to me that I could almost feel myself sitting in the car with her; experiencing the moment. The song played on.

Believe me the God of strength will never let you go.

The beauty of the message became the base of Noelle's journey. As I continued the walk and the story played out, I gave Noelle a home town of Atlanta, Georgia. No reason. Just as I typed that was what came out onto the paper. Later I began to look for the band to ask permission to use the beautiful words that they had created when I found out that they are from Alpharetta, Georgia, just north of Atlanta.

Why are we ever surprised when God directs our life? It only supports his plan and purpose for us.

How perfect that the only CD that could play in Noelle's car was from a local band. See how God in all of His wisdom masterminds even the fine details that encompass our lives. We have a God who wants to be in every area where we are.

So I say thank you to Steve Fee and the group. Your gift of music and your obedience to serve a living God with the talents that He has given you has now been used to send His message into the world of the written word. May the "Hand Of God" stretch forth and pour onto you His favor. And may your talents reach the world with His life changing message.

I am thankful for the connection that God joined in this written word. To Him be the glory.

Thank you,
Brenda Conley
Angel Wing Ministries

ACKNOWLEDGEMENTS

I owe all of my thanks and adoration to God who strengthens me and has opened the doors of the written word. May my life reflect who you want me to be and may I always stay in the purpose that you have for me. I always want to remain your humble servant.

Skip Coryell...you have been a life saver on this book. Without you and all of the work that you did to get me formatted, I would have cried many tears. Thank you.

Thank you to all of the brave women who were willing to share their experiences with me. Without you there would not have been this book. I am so proud of each and every one of you. Because of you, God allowed me to write this book. God began to drop each of you into my life and you opened your hearts and shared your pain and suffering. If through these words, one woman makes the decision to choose life for her baby then heaven will rejoice. God bless all of you as you walk towards a forgiving Father whose arms are stretched out wide. My prayer is that God will use this book to reach multitudes who think that they have only one way. That this will be a vessel for the broken who can't see past their sorrow. My hope is to strengthen young women before…

Ron, you gave me a card on our 36th wedding anniversary that said the Lord is your rock and your salvation. You said that He knew how much help you needed so He gave me to you. Then you spoke of your love for me and how it would be forever. I cried as I read the words that could have come right out of my own mouth. You spoke perfectly the thoughts that are in my heart. I will love you forever and ever. Thank you for loving me even when it's hard.

Josh, my first born, where have the years gone. I still remember so well the days of white curly hair, three piece suits and that twinkle in your eye as you kept us all laughing. I thank God for the brokenness that helped to create the man in you. Thank you for your solid strength and encouragement straight from God's Word. The Lord has an amazing calling on your life. Do not walk. Run into His arms and let Him lead you into those amazing songs that were designed before the foundations of the earth were created by the Master just for you to sing.

Melanie, a year a ago we couldn't have guessed what God had in story for our family. How he brought you to Josh and created heavenly music in the two of you was nothing more than God fulfilling the mission that He started in your lives many years ago. Then to watch as He joined you in love as He had created you to worship Him was so fun. To see the two of you happy and loving God together brings tears to my eyes. You voices blend with a perfection that only He could have purposed. Thank you again for adding to the completeness of our family.

Javan and Calli, how you just fit into the mix of this crazy group we call family. Poppi and I are so excited to watch you grow into who God created you to be. We are anxious to discover the beauty in you. You have both filled in a spot that was missing in our grandchildren and it has been years since I got to do girl things like dance recitals and hair play. Grow in God's goodness and walk in His ways as He stretches you into the spot that He made only for you to fill. We love you.

Levi, I love watching you desperate for Him and His truth. Your exuberance for the Lord has pushed us all closer. Your digging has opened doors to us that we didn't even know were there. Our God is the supernatural. Continue to teach us what is waiting for us to grasp. Show us how to unlock the mysteries of this life so that we can walk in all that the Lord has waiting for us. Use the gifts that He has given you; the world is full of broken people who need everything that you have to offer. Be humble. It was that spirit of Him in you that made you capable to be His.

Becky, as moms we look at our little ones and think that God has given us a complete family. It is not until our children are grown and married that we really see how God completes. You brought so many special gifts to this family. I stand amazed how God addresses every tiny detail. He knew that we would need a photographer. He knew that we would need someone who would be obedient to the call of home schooling. He knew that we would need a smart shopper. He knew that we would love to have someone to cook wonderful meals for us. He knew that we would need you. I am grateful for all that you do and I love you completely.

Gredin, Gavin, Gabriel and soon to be Gideon. Look at you. Wonderful young men. The kingdom of heaven was rejoicing the day that you were born. You are going to do amazing works for the Lord. We love watching you grow and seeing the special talents that God is developing in you. Gredin your artistic talent speaks out in everything that you do from the way that you look at the world that God created to the things that you draw. Gavin your soft spirit shows the love that you have for everyone. Your gentleness is going to reach so many for the Lord. Gabe at 3 1/2 you are such a gentle loving spirit. Nothing is too hard for you to try as you charge ahead. God has a world waiting for you to burst into… CHARGE! And we have Gideon. Who has God created you to be. We speak God's blessing on you and wait to see the spot that only you can fill.

Jessi, my daughter. You are so much like your Dad. Tough as nails with a briskness that hides a compassion and softness for the world. I wish that I could have seen you at work fighting to save lives of babies that are so tiny they barely fit in your hands. I can mentally see you totally focused on the task before you; determined to be victorious, as you cover up your breaking heart. Always the smallest with so much energy. Take time to see God's kingdom and all that He created for you. Your Dad and I are so proud of you. It was worth all of the battles of helping God shape your strong will. Know that God holds our babies for just a moment. Thank you God for your love. Your faithfulness stretches towards the heavens.

Brandon, it feels like you have always been a part of this family. From the time that you and Jessi were 16 and just starting to date we have watched the two of you develop into adults and now parents. Watching this journey has been a pleasure for us. Your determination to do this God's way has blessed all of us. See the humor of God in how He brought all of this together. Into a family of intense athletes He drops an artist who didn't play sports. However, don't you love His sense of humor? Imagine our astonishment when we saw that you probably are the best athlete of all of us. I still am thrilled that along with that comes your amazing artistic ability and your calm wisdom. Love my covers. Completeness…that is our God.

Ezekiel Jace as much as your mother is her dad, that much and more you are your mother. I remember the fits well. I also remember the frustrations and challenges. But, now I see where God took all of that in your momma's life. God must have some amazing things planned for your future that will put that strong willed personality to good use. Molding is never a fun process; but worth it in the end. You have been such a fighter from birth. We speak blessings over you as you fight to become who God created you to be. Poppi and I are eager to watch. The world waits for all that your personal hand print will touch. And the joy of your new brother, Judah Asher. He seems to be your opposite. As you are rough, he seems calm. What will you teach him? What gifts will he add to our family? We speak blessings on your lives.

Seth, I can only imagine what goes through your head as

you sit in the woods waiting patiently for the monstrous buck to pass your way. You know that you were that patient from birth. Into a crazy family you came at a time when we were least expecting God to bless us with a baby. In the middle of building a house, living out of boxes, with life going on all around us, you just quietly watched, so content, taking in everything. Are you that way in the woods? Is your head filled with thoughts of the messages that you have? Do you hear God's voice in the quiet? Never stop listening. God has blessed you with a gift to relate to the youth. Your relevance because of your young age will open so many doors to do His work. Go where He leads and reach them. They need you. And so does this family. Get ready God is about to change your life forever as we wait for "Baby Girl".

Kyleigh, two intense years of school and now you are done. Hoorah! How exciting! Have I told you how much fun it is to watch you play with the babies? To see a glimpse of who you will be as a mother in April. Your laugh is so contagious; to see their eyes light up when Auntie Ky comes. I have to say with a little jealousy that I think you are their favorite (although it is a close tie with Poppi). God's theme here seems to be completeness and I think of how well you complete Seth. Your patience matches his and adds another dimension on God's call for you to work with the youth. You brought another piece of the puzzle into our family and helped to complete the picture. We love you.

To all of you…God is why I write; but you my dear family are why I love. From the teachings of the past to the teachings of the future, we walk this life together and nothing will separate us from the Lord or each other.

All of my love,
Mom

STORY CHARACTERS

Naming the characters in my stories is like giving birth to my own children. I have always thought it important that they have strong names that will serve them well through life. I decided it was important that I share with you why I chose the names of the people that you will meet in this story.

Noelle--(French origin meaning "born at Christmas time) She is a broken 19 year old. The oldest daughter in what was supposed to be a wonderful family. If asked, they would tell you that they are Christians; however, Christmas, Easter and marriages sum up their church life experience as a family. Noelle and her sisters attended summer Vacation Bible School programs and you will see how the Word of God is faithful. You will walk with her through a life changing experience. See how God made a way for her through all of it. All she had to do was look at His hand guiding and directing her path.

Brad Conroy--(English origin meaning "one who has broad shoulders") A hard working 22 year old who's life is about to change as he follows his heart into an area of God's leading. Brad is faithful to wait upon the Lord and wise enough to honor his father and mother.

Eyan Conroy--(Gaelic origin; form of John meaning "God is gracious") Brad's brother. Twenty years old and ready to embrace the world. He is looking to branch out into the world of the unknown. Living on the farm is not in his future. His passion is to reach the lost for the Lord out on a mission field somewhere adventurous.

Angelina Conroy--(Greek form of Angela, meaning "a heavenly messenger; an angel") Her name really represents the part that she will play in Noelle's life. A survivor; full of wisdom and willing to walk through the ugliness of her past life to help save the life of an unborn child.

Genie Smith--(English origin; form of Jean meaning

“God is gracious”) Noelle’s mother. Trying to heal from a broken marriage. Her main focus becomes her girls.

Gale Smith--(Irish origin meaning a foreigner) This was the husband and father to Genie and their daughters. His leaving caused a hole in their family that left them trying to figure out who they are. He really did become a foreigner to them.

Debbie--(Hebrew origin; in the Bible a prophetess) Genie’s sister. She loves her sister and nieces and wants only to help support them.

Nissa--(Hebrew origin meaning “one who tests others”) The middle sister. Thrust into becoming the protector in the home. Loves her sisters desperately and is the peace maker in the family. Seventeen years old and starting her senior year of high school.

Anaya--(African origin meaning “One who looks up to God) The youngest of the three girls. Anaya and Noelle have the closest bond of the girls. She feels thc pain of Noelle the most. She is going to be sixteen.

Michael Dunn--(Hebrew origin meaning “Who is like God”) Genie’s boss. His life will be touched by watching this family walk through fire and come out on the other side with a deeper relationship with the Lord.

Michelle--(French origin and feminine form of Michael meaning “Who is like God“) She apart from anyone else will be able to come along side of Noelle. They will become friends through an understanding of brokenness.

Shawn--(Irish origin and a form of John, meaning “God is gracious.”) Shawn is laughter when times get hard. There is always a smile waiting from him.

These characters will follow each other through this book and into the next. Embrace them as they share the word of Jesus Christ with a waiting world.

FORWARD

I asked to write this foreword. I did this for me. This was another step in the healing process of my life. I did this to help heal the ugly scars in my life. No one knows about my secret except the dad.

I am one of the wounded. I've had two abortions. And it took me years of living in emotional turmoil to finally be able to accept the love of a Savior and believe that He could love me. I carried so much guilt about what I had done. I hated myself. My thinking was that surely God could not love me either.

I remembered every day the moments of those abortions. The sounds, the smells, the casual conversations that the doctor and nurse had while they were ripping my babies out of my body.

Why did I do it? The only answer I have is fear. I didn't want to let my parents down. Would they still love me? How would a baby change my life? What would people think?

If I only knew then, what I now know. The real fear was that I was going to have to live with the screams in the middle of the night when I would wake up reliving those moments; the fear of not knowing if I was going to go to hell; the fear of the unknown for my children.

Mentally I was haunted. What would my babies have looked like? Were they girls? Or were they boys? Did they know that the mother who was supposed to protect them was causing their death? These were real questions that I lived with every day.

It wasn't until I found the love of the Lord that I began to believe that I could be loved. He took away the nightmares. He answered my questions and brought peace into my life. He will do that for you too. Don't believe the lies. There are consequences to the choices that you make. And you will have to live with them. Life after abortion is hard. If they tell you different, they never had one.

— Anonymous —

INTRODUCTION

It was never my intention to be a great writer. I never dreamed of writing the world's best novel. I never gave much thought to words at all.

One day, in a cry of desperation and despair, I heard God's voice say, "Go, and write a book". You can only imagine my shock! First at hearing God's voice speak to me and second at His direction into an area that I had no knowledge.

I paused, "What?"

And God knowing that I would need affirmation said, "Go to the computer and write a book".

Though I am not always very good at being obedient, I did not question God a second time. I at least went to the computer and set in front of it.

"What now Lord? I don't know how to write a book."

He said, "Write what you know."

So I did. I sat at the computer and wrote. And my first book came out of that obedience.

Being the control freak that I am, I decided that this wasn't so hard. I researched it and discovered how I should have done it and set about preparing to write my second book.

One day at 5:00 a.m. the Lord woke me up and told me to go and write the second book. I went. This time I was totally prepared. Knew what I was going to write. Pulled out all of my notes and my outline, ready to begin the way that I had now learned was the correct way to write a book.

God had another plan. I began to type and the story that unfolded on the computer was about people that I didn't know and a story that I hadn't thought about. But the book was done, printed, and released at a conference for girls in the span of one month. When God has a plan, He gives you what you need to accomplish the task that He has called you to do. The third book was a whisper in my ear from God. One night as I watched my Mom in her bed as the angels prepared to take her home to be with the Lord, God said, "this is the third book and you'll call it 'WHEN THE ANGELS CAME'." So I wrote the third book. I had just finished that book when I felt the whisper of God about the next book. Not quite as clear; but He was laying it into my heart in bits and pieces. I wasn't sure about His direction. I wasn't the person to write this book. I argued with Him some. He said, "With Me all things are possible. I will never leave you or forsake you. My burden is light. My yoke is easy." Okay Lord I get it. For just a moment I took my eyes off of You and began to see through my eyes." So this is my fourth book. And I write where He leads me. I wait on His direction. I walk in His understanding. He is all knowing. He gives what we need when we need it. HE IS THE GREAT OMNIPOTENT (by the way, the dictionary tell us that means--having unlimited power or authority--all-powerful). So, all I have to do is write and He will give me what I need to finish the project that He has called me to do. So…here goes. I hope that this book makes a difference in your life. I hope that it is life changing, if that's what you need. I hope that you feel His love. For He IS a loving God and nothing IS too big to separate us from His love. He will forgive anything and anyone who calls on His name. Otherwise, He sent His Son, Jesus, to the cross for nothing. And God wouldn't have done that. He sent his Son to the cross for you and for me. The cost He paid is priceless. He loved us that much. His love endures forever and ever. By His grace we will carry on. Amen and Amen.

Chapter One

PSALM 116:1-6
I love the LORD, for He heard my voice;
He heard my cry for mercy.
Because He turned His ear to me,
I will call on Him as long as I live.
The cords of death entangled me,
the anguish of the grave came upon me;
I was overcome by trouble and sorrow.
Then I called on the name of the LORD;
"O LORD, save me!"
The Lord is gracious and righteous,
our God is full of compassion.
The LORD protects the simple hearted;
when I was in great need, He saved me."

AS IT RAINED

THE WATER POURED DOWN MATCHING THE TEARS THAT flowed from her eyes. The windshield wipers swooshed, back and forth, back and forth in rhythm to the music by a group called "FEE" that played from her CD player: It was in the car that she had just purchased. It wasn't what she would have chosen to listen to; but the radio didn't work and it was all that she had. So she played it. She needed noise; something to take her jumbled mind off of her circumstances.

> *"I know it seems like this could be the darkest day you know.*

The words from the CD spoke to her heart as it broke, shattered in a way that she knew could never be put back together again.

Believe me the God of strength will never let
you go.

She so wanted to believe that was true. He was supposed to be like a daddy right? She needed a Daddy whose arms she could climb into and be cradled and rocked. She wanted to feel the warmth of someone who loved her. She was so cold…chilled to the bone inside and out. She felt like she was so far away from the warmth that she would never feel it again.

He will overcome. I know.

No one knows. She knew that for sure. No one could understand where she was now. She was lost and alone. Alone, for the first time in her life. Desperate. She was on the run. By herself. With no one to save her. Not from her running or from her thoughts. The CD played on.

And the arms that hold the universe are
holding you tonight. You can rest inside.
It's going to be all right.
And the voice that calmed the raging sea is
calling you His child.

Rest. There was no rest. Only running. No one's voice to calm the raging that was going on inside of her.

So be still and know that He is in control.
He will never let you go.

She let go. She had to. It was the only way that she could protect those that she loved. It would hurt too much if she had stayed. They would all have to forget. At least for a time. Why did it have to hurt this much? Maybe someday she could go back; or maybe not. What if they all forgot? The business of everyday life would begin to fill in the empty spaces and life would just roll along until one day became another; one year would become another. But, if she had stayed, the hurt might have been manifested into an everyday reminder. No… this way was best. This way would hurt less. This way only she would know. This way she had time to figure out what was next. Her mind was so torn between what was right and what was wrong.

Through many dangers, toils and snares you
have all ready come.

She cried more as she thought about the dangers that she had toyed with. The dangers that had brought her to this moment. Snares…that was a good word to describe what she had walked through. She had been snared. And the consequences were…well they were this. This moment that she was now in.

His grace has brought you safe this far.
His grace will lead you home.

She couldn't go home. She had to stay away, maybe forever, so that she could protect them; she loved her mom and sisters that much.

And the arms that hold the universe are
holding you tonight.
You can rest inside.
It's going to be all right.
And the voice that calmed the raging sea
is calling you His child.
So be still and know that He is in control.
He will never let you go.

More tears. She had cried for so long. It seemed like days. Her eyes were so swollen and red. They burned continually.

"This is your life now." She would say it out loud as a reminder to herself. If she said it over and over, maybe she would accept where her life was going. Forget. Forget. That was what she had to do. If she could forget what she had lost, it would be easier to accept where she was now.

You can hope
You can rise
You can stand.
Still got the world in His hands.
You can hope
You can rise
You can stand.
Still got the world in His hands.

No hope. I have no hope. I can't rise. I can't stand and He won't hold my world. Not now. I'm too far away now. There isn't any going back. I'm going forward. By myself. This is my fault. I will take responsibility and I'll live with the consequences. I will not cause them grief because of my decisions.

And the arms that hold the universe are
holding you tonight.
You can rest inside.
It's going to be alright.
And the voice that calmed the raging sea
is calling you His child.
So be still and know that He is in control.
He will never let you go.

I have to be in control now. As soon as I figure out what to do; I have to be strong. As soon as I figure out how to do that; I'll find a way. I will…because I have to.

How did I get here, she wondered? "The blessed life", isn't that how people had referred to her life. The oldest daughter of three girls; with a little more than a year between each of them; it seemed to be the perfect family. A close family. There was always laughter and love in her home. Everyone had a place and as unusual as it may seem there never was a place for jealousy. The girls were best friends. They could talk about everything. They shared their most intimate feelings; from their fears as children to the questions of maturing. An open home. That would be a good way to describe their home. A home that represented a safe haven in a world gone crazy. Noelle loved to come home.

No more now. No more would she go home and share the laughter and love. No more would she go home to the smell of homemade bread and soup cooking on the stove. Her favorite was always the bean soup. No more would Mom ask her how her day had been. Then patiently wait as she told word for word what had happened. Mom was always such a great listener. She really cared what you had to say. No more would she sit on her bed after her shower and talk with her sisters, Nissa and Anaya, with their heads wrapped in towels. No more would they talk of nonsense and foolishness leading to fits of laughter while they waited for the polish to dry on their toes. No more would she sleep in the warmth of her own bed and wake to the sounds so familiar to her. No more would she feel safe and secure. No more.

The tears continued to flow. Surely the breaking sound of her heart was loud enough to be heard. But who could hear it. She was on her own. There was no one else to hear; no one else to sooth her sorrow. No one.

Chapter Two

PSALM 139:9-12
If I rise on the wings of the dawn,
if I settle on the far side of the sea,
even there Your hand will guide me,
Your right hand will hold me fast.
If I say, "Surely the darkness will hide me
and the light become night around me,"
even the darkness will not be dark to You;
the night will shine like the day,
for darkness is as light to You.

The Accident

As the rain continued to fall and the day darkened to night, Noelle's mind wandered to just a year ago. Before…before everything changed. She would love to go back and play that last year over. They had no idea. It took them all by surprise, shock would describe it better. There were no warning signs. Nothing that threw up red flags. One day they were the perfect family and then the emptiness consumed them. The laughter in their home died and that space was filled with silence. You know, the kind of silence that makes you hurt. It's a physical pain and it's a very real pain.

Noelle still remembers coming home after school. The day had been just an average day. Nothing outstanding. Nothing that would have said that her life was about to morph into something that she wouldn't even recognize.

Looking back she knew something was wrong as soon as

she walked into the house. Her sisters had beat her home and she could hear weeping. It was the kind of crying, almost a yell, that made you feel like something was being ripped out of you. Her stomach rose into her throat. She could taste the bile that was rising up. Something was terribly wrong. Funny how now she can even recognize the smells of that day. Though she didn't notice it then; now she can remember that there was the smell of pot roast in the slow cooker. There would be potatoes and those little mini carrots. Mom would have made her awesome gravy. They should have set down to the table with salad and always a little something sweet to end the meal with. There would have been laughing as they all discussed what had happened in their day.

But instead Noelle walked into a living room of sorrow. There sat her mom holding Nissa and Anaya as they cried. No one seemed to notice me through their sobbing. I had to yell a second time, "What's wrong?"

As they looked up, I realized that it had to be Dad. My hero. The man who was my defender and protector. Something terrible must have happened to him. Why else would everyone be so heart broken. I began to cry before they even explained. I knew that nothing that they said at this point was going to fix what was wrong.

Mom looked up. The look on her face was old. I knew that whatever it was had just aged my beautiful mother. She stood and so did my sisters. They came and wrapped their arms around me.

I was yelling, "No!...No!...What is wrong?...Where is Dad?"

Then those words from my mom that changed my life, "Your dad has left us," Mom said as she broke into another round of tears.

I didn't understand. "Left us? Left us for what? Heaven? Left us? Where did he go? Is he dead?" My sister hands me a letter. I can see that it is Dad's hand writing. But the words that are on that paper can't be from Dad. Not from my dad. He wouldn't be writing these words. We are the perfect family. We are so lucky. Things like this don't happen to us. Things like this happen to other people. People who have a different life than we have. People who have problems. Not us.

I read his words as they blur on the paper. He says, "I know that this is going to hurt all of you. But I hope that someday you will be able to forgive me. I never planned for this to happen. It just did. I have tried to pretend that I could continue on as things are; but it isn't working. I am going away to start a new life. Please forgive me. I will always love each of you. But understand that I can't live the rest of my life without the new love that I have found. If I could do things differently, I would. My heart is very sad. I love you. Dad.

I'm screaming now. My sisters are screaming too. I realize that my mom is on the floor. We all fall to the floor and we are rocking and crying.

We are still there the next morning when the sun comes up. I don't know what happened to the night. What I do know is that a part of our family died that day and left a hole that can't be filled.

We never heard from that man again. There was an attorney who handled all of his correspondences. As a family, we were never given the opportunity to voice our anger. We were never given the opportunity to say good-bye. We were never offered that moment to ask why. One day we were a family and the next day it was just over. All that was left was cleaning it up and making it all tidy for him. Oh, he made sure that we were taken care of. He gave my mom the house that we had always lived in and there is a check that comes to our house every month from the same attorney that was so business like. But our life changed and it seems to continue to spiral down hill for me. I have anger; almost hatred in a spot that used to hold a love that overflowed. I guess that will define me forever from that day on.

Noelle's tears for that moment in time and the tears for the moment that she was in now mingle together. They become the same sorrows. She can see that what happened that day led her into decisions that caused her to be where she is at this moment. But that doesn't change anything. She still has to do what she is doing. The pain of the last year has left her no options. Her mom and sisters don't deserve to carry more burdens. And she certainly won't be the person that inflicts them with more pain.

Suddenly, there is a big bang that interrupts her thoughts. Her car begins to sway to and fro on the road; from one side to the next and back. Noelle turned the wheel one way and then the other. With the car out of control and the mix of the wet roads, she was sure that the car was going to roll. But it didn't and somehow she got it to stop on the side of the road.

Her heart was pumping. The fear began to overtake her. "What am I supposed to do now?" she cried out. Cried out to whom? She didn't know. And certainly no one was answering her. She laid her head down on the steering wheel. The tears flowed harder if that was even possible. For what seemed like hours she cried. Until there were no more tears she cried. Then she slept.

The dreariness of the morning confused her as she opened her eyes. She only knew it was morning because her watch told her it was. The rain was still falling. Would it never stop raining? She had to do something. She couldn't just sit here along the side of the road forever. There didn't seem to be a lot of traffic. She had purposefully taken back roads. She wasn't even sure if a car had passed by while she slept. She must have slept hard.

She had carefully planned so that it would be impossible to

find her. She was in a car that no one would connect with her. It was a simple car, nothing that would stand out in a crowd. A silver Buick Skylark. It was an older car; but had been owned by a little old grandma who seldom drove. Noelle had paid cash for the car and had handled all of the arrangements by herself. She really thought herself quite cleaver. She had tried to think of anything that would trip her up and allow them a way to find her. Noelle had purchased a Post Office box and had all of her mail delivered there. Then she told the Postmaster that she would be leaving town and that she would send a forwarding address as soon as she had one. She contacted all agencies that were important and gave them her new address. After dropping her classes at the university, she used a Secretary of State's Office in another town to purchase the car and she found a different insurance agent than her mother uses.

She purchased the car on her way out of town and she didn't look back. It had been simple to pack her things. The timing was perfect. The sisters and Mom had decided to go out of town to visit her Aunt Debbie. They had been planning the trip for a couple of weeks and that gave Noelle time to set her plan into action. They had begged Noelle to go with them. She had almost backed down and said yes. She would have loved just one more trip with them. Some more time to build up memories to last her for a lifetime if that was what needed to happen. But she had to remain strong. After all, she was being given a great opportunity to line everything up. It would be four days before they would return; four days before they would know that she was gone. Long gone; possibly a lifetime gone.

Noelle used the excuse that she had too much homework for a college class where she was struggling. They believed that. It had been a hard year for all of them to focus on the everyday things. So they said good-bye. Hugs and kisses all around. Noelle was strong until they pulled out of the driveway and then she slid down the door and allowed herself some time to cry as she closed the door on this past life. All she could think about was how much she loved them. She wouldn't allow herself time to think about how much she was going to miss them. Not now. There would be time for that after she was on the road. Now she had to pick up the car, pack up her belongings, pull what money she had in her savings out of the bank and drive away from what she knew.

The letter had been a process. She had started it when she began to put her plan together. She had finished it two nights ago.

Noelle hated that she was saying good-bye in a letter. She remembered the ugliness of leaving a letter. It was a coward's way out. Just like her dad. But there didn't seem to be a better way. His was the cleanest. They would have less of a chance of tracking her. A phone call could be tracked. Plus, she knew that she wouldn't be able to stay strong if she heard their voices once she had left. No a letter was the only way.

By 11:30 a.m. she was on the road. The car seemed to drive itself. All she knew was that she was headed north. She chose north because they knew that her dad was living in the south. The attorney had let that slip one day. She assumed that when they looked for her they would start in that direction. So she went north.

Now here she was stranded on the side of a dirt road three days later. One more day and her family would be home and they would find the note. She had hoped that by then she would have put as much distance between them as she could. So first things first, she had to figure out what was wrong with the car before she could make her next decision. Slipping into a hooded sweatshirt and stepping into the rain, Noelle moved like an aged person feeling the fatigue that was starting to wash over her.

The rain was falling softly. Not the hard pouring rain that she had driven in for the last three days; just the kind of rain that seems to cleanse. Looking up into the sky, she let the rain wash over her. It felt good to have water on her face. Her eyes were so swollen and dry from crying that the rain soothed them. She stood for minutes as the falling water was washing away the tear tracks.

Her car was front wheel drive and there was the problem. The front tire on the driver's side was flat. As in destroyed flat. That tire wasn't going to carry this car anywhere; even if she knew where anywhere was. Which she didn't.

Noelle got back into the car. She closed and locked all of the doors and set there shivering. What was she going to do now? She was too weary to think one more minute. Sleep for now…just sleep. As her eyes slowly closed, the darkness of her life consumed her and she allowed the weariness to take her to a place where everything was all right.

CHAPTER 3

PSALM 33:6-11
By the word of the LORD
were the heavens made,
their starry host by the breath of His mouth.
He gathers the waters of the sea into jars;
He puts the deep into storehouses.
Let all the earth fear the LORD;
let all the people of the world revere Him.
For He spoke, and it came to be;
He commanded, and it stood firm.
The LORD foils the plans of the nations;
He thwarts the purposes of the people.
But the plans of the LORD
stand firm forever,
the purposes of His heart
through all generations

A LOST SOUL

BRAD WAS ON HIS WAY HOME FROM HIS MORNING COLLEGE classes. On Mondays he only had two morning classes and then he had the rest of the day to try to catch up on things that needed to get done on the farm. Maybe catch up was the wrong phrase to use. The work on the farm was never caught up. And if he got close, there was always work at the restaurant to do. It was while he was making his plans for the rest of the day that he saw the car along the side of the road. He thought it a little strange to see a car that he didn't know sitting where it was. This was a pretty deserted road.

It wasn't very often that a car passed by that wasn't known to those who lived here. He made a mental note of the out of state license plate and was simply going to call the police and report it. He saw that it had a flat tire. It looked like the tire had blown out hard.

However, as he passed by he noticed that the driver was a young girl. She couldn't be much older than he was. Her head was lying back on the seat and he became concerned. He decided to stop and make sure that everything was okay.

Pulling his truck over and getting out, Brad walked slowly up to the car. As crazy as it was to think that something out of the way would happen on this quiet stretch of rural road, he still decided to approach with caution. After two knocks on the window and no response, he wasn't sure what to do next. Something in his spirit did a little check. So he knocked one more time and shouted, "Hey!"

At that Noelle raised her head and startled at the sight of a man standing outside of her car door. As her head cleared, fear rushed through her. There was nothing good about any of this. Here she was a girl by herself in a car that wasn't going anywhere with a man by himself on an empty road. What if he had a gun? She decided to appear fearless. Somewhere she remembered watching a National Geographic show about bears, or was it dogs, that said they can smell fear. Apparently that was a bad thing.

Brad was relieved when she finally raised her head. Although, concern rose within him; she looked like someone who had been punched hard in the face. Her eyes were swollen almost shut and very red. There were black smudges of what he guessed to be eye makeup all over her face. And her hair was a mess. She looked like an abused child and he couldn't even guess her age. Yet there was a hidden beauty somewhere behind all of the sorrow. He didn't even know how he knew it was sorrow; but he did.

He could see that she was startled by the roll of emotion that passed across her face. With the mess that faced him he almost laughed when, with all of the dignity she could muster, she announced that she was fine and did not need any assistance. She gave him a 'thank you' almost as if dismissing him. Then turned and looked straight ahead as if to say, "You may leave now."

Brad wasn't sure what to do next. He asked, "Are you sure? Do you know that you have a flat tire and that your car isn't going anywhere? I live just up the road with my mom and brother. You are more than welcome to come with me and we'll see about getting you another tire."

"Thank you for the offer. However, I am quite capable of helping myself." She stated leaving Brad nothing more to do than continue on to his house.

"Okay suit yourself. If you change your mind, our house is about one mile down this road. That's a long walk in the rain; which by the way isn't supposed to stop anytime soon. But if you aren't going to let me help you, there isn't any reason for me to stand out here and get wet any longer. If you change your mind, my name is Brad Conroy."

Brad tipped his hat as he walked back to his truck. A little unsure about what had just happened, he shook his head wondering what she thought that she was going to do to fix that tire. He had lived in these parts his whole life and he knew that there wasn't any place within twenty miles that was going to come out here with a new tire. That was, if she even had a cell phone that would have any kind of service in this area to call anyone.

What was really bothering him was the way that she looked. She was in need of something. Just what that was he wasn't sure. Yet, he knew that he had done all that he could for the time being. So he stepped into his truck and drove away. Still he found himself looking into his rear view mirror wondering about the sad little girl woman he had just left behind. Who was she? And why was she all the way out here? Where was she running to or who was she running from?

He would call his mom when he got home and explain the situation to her. Maybe she would have some suggestions that he hadn't thought of. Still his mind went round and round about the person sitting back there in the car so sad and looking so frightened behind that false shell. His heart was hurting for this total stranger. And he couldn't understand why. Unless it was because she was one of God's broken creatures and Brad liked to fix things. Was God going to put her into Brad's life for a short period of time? Brad knew that the Heavenly Father had all of the answers that Brad didn't have so he threw up a quick prayer on her behalf.

God, You have a daughter in trouble. She will not let me help her. If it is Your will, can You open a door so that I could help her. One thing is for sure, she needs You, whether she knows it or not. Amen.

Brad went into the house and straight to the phone to call his mother. She was working at the restaurant that she owned. He waited as one of the girls went to get her. Apparently she was out on the floor waiting tables today. Must be that someone was absent. He thought to himself.

"Bradley, you had better talk quickly. We are so busy and I am trying to fill two pairs of shoes today. One of the girls is going to be off indefinitely. Ally fell and broke her ankle last night. I guess that she slipped in the mud and twisted it wrong. So what's up?" Brad's mom talked about as fast as any one man could listen. But listening was her specialty. As he told her the story, she was reading between the lines. She could also hear the sadness that was in his voice. She knew that it was really bothering him that the girl had not allowed him to help her. If she was in as big of a mess as Brad described, then maybe trusting men wasn't something that came easy to her. Still there had to be a way that they could help. She thought for just a minute and came up with a plan. Quite a good plan if she did say so herself.

"Brad, listen to me, here is what I want you to do." She continued to explain to him what seemed like a great idea.

"Thanks Mom. I think that I'll start getting everything ready as soon as I get off of the phone. I'm sorry about Ally. I assume that means that you will be late tonight?" Brad asked.

"I hope not. I'm already tired just thinking about the days ahead. I'll be home as soon as I can. Let me know how everything turns out." She replied as she hung up on her end.

CHAPTER 4

PSALM 107:1-9
Give thanks to the LORD, for He is good;
His love endures forever.
Let the redeemed of the LORD say this—those He redeemed
from the hand of the foe,
those He gathered from the lands,
from east and west, from north and south.
Some wandered in desert wastelands,
finding no way to a city where they could settle.
They were hungry and thirsty, and their lives ebbed away.
Then they cried out to the LORD in their trouble,
and He delivered them from their distress.
He led them by a straight way to a city
where they could settle.
Let them give thanks to the LORD for His unfailing love
and His wonderful deeds for men, for He satisfies the thirsty
and fills the hungry with good things

FEEDING THE BODY AND SOUL

NOELLE WAS RELIEVED THAT THE MAN WAS GONE FOR A brief moment. She sighed as he drove away. But, that still left her with the problem of the tire. What was she going to do? Here she set with no way to call a wrecker for assistance. And whom would she call anyway if she had a phone. She purposely hadn't taken her phone with her when she left. She wasn't going to take the chance of being tracked through the use of her cell phone.

She didn't even know where she was. She didn't have a

plan when she left. Just driving north and staying off main roads. That was her plan. So she started off north and then just made turns as she went. She had no idea what town or even what state she was in. What she did know was that she was tired; she was hungry; and she hadn't seen a restroom for longer than she wanted to remember. The last time that she stopped to fill up the car she had grabbed a cup of coffee and a bag of corn chips with a cheese stick. She had quickly used the bathroom. She looked so bad that she hadn't wanted to draw attention to herself. Because of that she chose to avoid restaurants or places where too many people would see her. She wore sunglasses and a hat anytime that she left the car. Now the rain was getting to be a real problem. She realized that she hadn't asked if there was a spare tire in the trunk. And if there was, could she change the tire herself. They had briefly walked through that in drivers training a few years go. She hadn't really paid attention during that lesson. She wasn't ever going to have to deal with that. She had her dad. He would always take care of that kind of stuff for her. Well guess what, life changes. Now there's no one to count on but herself.

Noelle got out of the car and stepped into the trees for a quick moment. She had to admit that she was a little spooked. There were little noises everywhere. You would think that all creatures would tuck away during the rain.

With that done she opened the trunk and didn't see anything that resembled a tire. Now what? Back into the car and out of the rain to think.

One thing was for sure, she couldn't stay here all day and through the night again. That guy would certainly think something was up. The last thing that she needed was to have him call the police.

At just that moment, she saw the familiar truck coming towards her. Panic flushed through her. She didn't have anywhere to go. So she sat and repeated in her head, "Don't let them smell fear. Don't let them smell fear." As she continued to repeat the phrase, Brad Conroy stopped the truck directly across from her car and rolled down his window. He motioned for her to do the same.

Noelle looked at him wondering if he could be trusted. The thought was flowing through her head that he could have gone and got a gun and there would be nothing that she could do to stop him from hurting her. The fear from a similar situation began to surface from somewhere deep inside. She swallowed those thoughts away. She never wanted to think about that night again. That was before and this was now. Now she would be determined. She would be in charge. So she cracked the window just a little. Enough so that she could talk to him; but not enough so that he could grab at her.

Brad spoke, "It occurred to me that you may be hungry. My mom owns a restaurant in town about 20 miles east of here so we always have great food in the kitchen. I put together a plate. It's still warm and you are welcome to it. There is even homemade apple pie. If you like chocolate better though, there's also a brownie that I promise will be the best that you have ever eaten. I would have heated it up and put ice cream on top; but I couldn't figure out how I could keep the cream from melting."

The smell was wafting over into the car and already Noelle's stomach was doing flip flops just thinking about putting real food in it again. She wanted to be strong and refuse the food that was being offered; but she couldn't. All of the sudden Noelle realized that she was starving. He offered the plate of food one more time and the window was down as she was taking the delicious smelling food into her car.

The window went up as she tore the cover off the plate. There was a feast before her. Country fried chicken, mashed potatoes and gravy, baked beans and the best looking corn bread muffin she had ever seen. She grabbed the plastic silverware and started shoveling the food into her mouth. In her sadness, she hadn't even realized the hunger that was gripping her. After all she wasn't just feeding herself. She was feeding a baby that was growing inside of her; a mass of cells that she didn't want and hadn't asked for. There was this thing that had changed her life. There was a problem that had caused her to run from the home that she loved. It had taken away from her the only family that she had left. This baby wasn't welcome to stay in her body. It was going to be gone as soon as she could figure out how to make that happen.

But for now, she would eat; savoring the delicious taste of food brought by a man that she did not trust. He was right though; the brownie was the best she had ever eaten. She knew because she ate the brownie right after she had eaten the apple pie.

CHAPTER 5

PSALM 37:23-29
If the LORD delights in a man's way,
He makes his steps firm;
Though he stumble, he will not fall,
for the LORD upholds him with His hand.
I was young and now I am old, yet I have never seen the
righteous forsaken or their children begging bread.
They are always generous and lend freely;
their children will be blessed.
Turn from evil and do good;
then you will dwell in the land forever.
For the LORD loves the just
And will not forsake His faithful one

THE FIRST TRUST STEP

BRAD WAS EXCITED THAT SHE HAD ACCEPTED THE PLATE OF food. By the way that she devoured everything that he had brought, he was sure that it had been a long time since she had eaten. Where had this girl come from? Who had broken her?

Brad asked God, *Father, what next?* as he watched her eat. She didn't even seem to remember that he was there. Her total focus as on the food that was in front of her. She didn't look up until every bite and every crumb was wiped away from the plate. Pie and brownie. That was okay with him. He was glad to have this moment to really study her. She had fine bone structure. And a short natural cut to her hair, wavy hair maybe. He thought that the color was dark blonde with a hint of red. He wanted to see into her eyes to discover their color. But those eyes were still so swollen and red that he couldn't get a good look.

At that point it must have occurred to her that he was watching. She looked up and smiled, "Thank you…I mean… for the food…that was…very kind of you. I am…sorry. My behavior must seem strange to you. I really do have better manners than this."

Brad was speechless. As she spoke his stomach began to feel funny; there was warmth that was spreading through his chest. And the thought occurred to him that he had never felt this way before. What was up with this; all of this just because a girl had spoken to him. He had spoken to girls his whole life. In fact he had never understood the big deal that his friends had made about girls. It wasn't that he didn't like girls. He did. He just thought that God was waiting to bring just the right girl his way.

He wondered, *God is this what it feels like to be attracted to someone?* He realized that from the first moment that he had set eyes on this girl urchin there had been a protective feeling that was welling up inside of him. It's crazy to imagine that you could have an immediate reaction to someone that you know nothing about; not even her name.

Well that had better be where he goes next. So he says, "You're welcome. It really was nothing. All I did was throw it onto a plate. And with the wonders of microwave here it is. I'm glad that you enjoyed it so much though. My mother will be too. She loves to hear that people like her cooking. Most people would say that she's the best cook around these parts."

Brad continued, "I feel at a disadvantage. You know my name; but I don't know yours. Would that be all right with you if I called you by your first name…which is…what?"

Noelle couldn't help but smile as Brad's face turned into an impish grin with two huge dimples.

"Don't think that I don't see right through your little trick Mr. Brad Conroy. You just want me to tell you my name. Well it doesn't happen just that easily. You will have to guess my name. It's a secret that only few know and I'm not allowed to divulge." Noelle hadn't given any thought to giving out her name. She wasn't sure that she should use her real name; but she hadn't thought of a different name just yet.

Brad offered a compromise. "How about we make a deal? I'll help you fix the tire on your car and as payment you'll tell me the secret."

Noelle relaxed as she found herself letting down her guard with the man who seemed to be able to make her laugh.

"Okay," she said. "But you have to promise me that you will not share the secret with anyone without my permission or I will have to turn you into a toad and run away."

Brad promised as he crossed his heart with his fingers. Yet he checked the thought that even in jest her thoughts were to run away. He was more convinced than ever that she was doing just that. This little urchin was on the run from something or someone and he intended to win her trust enough so that she would confide in him. For some reason that even he didn't understand, that was very important to him. He wanted to know her story. He wanted to know all about her. There was a deep desire to fill in all of the missing pieces. And those who knew him knew that Brad Conroy loved a challenge.

Brad asked if he could look in her trunk for a tire. Noelle told him that she had already looked. But that he was welcome to look again. She popped the trunk from the inside and waited as he checked. She could hear him moving things around and then he was at the side of her door again.

"There's a donut in the bottom of the trunk." He said.

"Well I don't know how a donut would have gotten in there. The trunk was empty when I packed it and I haven't bought any donuts along the way." She was confused when he started to laugh. She had to admit that she like the sound of his laughter. It was confident and sure. She thought, "This is a man secure in who he is. There's something different about him. Something that she couldn't put her finger on. If it had been a different circumstance or time, she would have liked to have spent more time trying to discover who he really is."

He stopped laughing. Then smiling at her said, "A donut refers to a small tire used as a spare for just a short period of time. It's only made to get you to a near place so that you can get a new tire."

"Oh…I see. The joke is on me."

"It is. However, the truth is that you are going to need a new tire. Now this is your best option as I see it. About twenty miles east is the small town of Willington. That's where my mom's restaurant is. There's a station there that can get you a tire for your car. He may have to order your tire in. It would probably be tomorrow before he would have it." Brad was watching the questions float across her face. He could tell that she was unsure about where he was going with all of this.

He continued with caution, "Now, I'm not sure that you're up to a trip into town. And I certainly don't want to pressure you into anything that you aren't comfortable doing right now. So understand that this is just a suggestion. I told you earlier that my home is a mile down this road. I live here with my mom and my younger brother. You're welcome to come and stay the night. We have extra bedrooms. You can shower and sleep and by tomorrow we can have your car ready to roll. What do you think?" Brad paused to allow her time to process all of this through. He could see that she was struggling with yes or no. He took note of her features as the questions and scenarios played out across her face. This was a girl woman who would not be very good at concealing secrets. Her face was easy to read. You could tell that she didn't like to depend on other people. Either she had always had to be tough or someone had hurt her terribly.

"Listen," Brad said. "Would you feel better if I called my mom so she can tell you that we aren't axe murderers and that I'm as honest as the day is long? She would tell you that and much more in a short length of time. She's quite the talker, you better be ready to listen fast."

Noelle had to smile at the description Brad gave of his mother. He said it in such an endearing way that you could feel the love that he had for her. She paused as sadness washed over her at the thought of what her mother was going to be doing soon. But she couldn't think about that; not now anyway.

What was it that she had always heard, "You can always tell the character of a man by the way that he treats his mother." If that was true, then she should be perfectly safe at Brad's house. Besides…what were her options? She took a look in the car mirror and knew instantly that she couldn't go into town and she was very tired. A shower would be wonderful.

"Okay, I'll go to your home and thank you for being so kind. I promise that I won't be a nuisance. And I will pay for every penny that this will cost. I'm not broke." Immediately she wondered if she should have said that. What if he thought that she had money and he wasn't as kind as she first thought?

Brad laughed out loud. In his heart of hearts he just knew that this girl was going to be anything but a nuisance. In fact, somewhere deep inside, there was excitement bubbling up in a way that he couldn't even describe.

"If I were you, I wouldn't go around town broadcasting that you have money. Not everyone you meet will be as nice as I am. This was just your lucky day." Chucking he said, "Come on…let's get you to a warm shower while I take care of this tire situation."

She unlocked the door and Brad opened it for her to exit. "What do you need to take with you?" He asked.

Noelle grabbed her purse and a small suitcase. "Just

these," she said.

Helping her step up into the passenger seat of his truck, he watched as she positioned her suitcase between them almost like a protective shield. It made him want to chuckle again. He didn't though. Instead he told her that he needed to copy down the numbers on her tire so that he could get the right tire ordered. Then he closed the truck door.

Noelle watched as he assuredly took care of the needs of the tire. He then opened her car door, took out her keys and pushed the locks to secure the car. Getting into the truck, he handed her the keys.

Smiling at her he asked, "Are you ready to go?"

"Yes", she answered and couldn't help being thankful for the goodness of this man.

He shifted into drive and headed down the road until he came to a track that entered a field. He didn't miss the emotion that flashed across her face as she realized that they were pulling into a secluded spot. Immediately he realized where her thoughts had gone and he said, "We'll turn around here and be home in a jiffy".

Of course they would have to turn around. The road was too small to maneuver this big truck. However, she did acknowledge that he had instantly been aware of her unease and had taken the time to reassure her without her saying a word. As they drove past her car, he told her that the car would be safe. "We don't see many strangers around these parts." He said.

Again, Noelle was thankful and had thoughts of peace. She wondered if this Brad Conroy had that affect on everyone.

CHAPTER 6

PSALM 130:1-6
Out of the depths I cry to You, O LORD;
O LORD, hear my voice.
Let Your ears be attentive to my cry for mercy.
If You, O LORD, kept a record of sins,
O LORD, who could stand?
But with You there is forgiveness;
therefore You are feared.
I wait for the LORD, my soul waits,
And in His word I put my hope.
My soul waits for the LORD
More than watchmen wait for the morning,
More than watchmen wait for the morning.

ANXIOUSLY WAITING

Genie, Noelle's mom, listens as the phone continues to ring and six rings later goes again to voice mail. She debates about leaving another message for her oldest daughter. She thinks about tomorrow when they will be back home. Leaving another message on day three seems futile. She consoles herself with the thought that probably her daughter has left her phone somewhere and can't access it. It wouldn't be unusual for that to happen. One of the girls is always looking for their phone. The girls all have their own phones, courtesy of their dad who seems to think that as long as he sends money to make sure that their life is comfortable, then he's doing his part. Well not true. The girls need him and as angry as it makes her to admit it, so does she.

A year later, divorce final and working at a job that she really does enjoy, still Genie spends hours reliving their life. She spends time wondering, was it her fault? Was there something that she could have done differently? Gale seemed to be a happy man. He was driven to be successful; and he was. He had worked hard to prepare himself for the kind of job that would supply enough wealth to live the life that he had always wanted. They were more than comfortable. Genie had never had to work and that was Gale's choice as much as it was hers. She loved being a stay at home wife and mother. She loved heading up committees in the community and contributing. Her family was her life. It brought her great joy to make a home for them. She loved fixing the special meals that she always prepared and gathering her family around the table every night. She especially loved the laughter. Gale was so attentive to their needs. Who would have guessed that he was unhappy? She was just as surprised as the people looking in from the outside were.

If she were to admit it, that fact alone causes her so much anger. It made her look stupid. That isn't who she is. It wasn't that she couldn't have made a name for herself in the outside world. She had always excelled. All through college she was the girl that was voted the most likely to succeed. She was pretty and smart; there was an excitement about her that brought others to her. People wanted to be where she was. Gale used to tell her that people were drawn to her like moths to a bright light. He would say that she sucked him in and he couldn't even help himself and that together they would make an inexorable pair. They were unstoppable and the world was just waiting to grant their wishes.

What happened? How did it all go so wrong? How could a man who professed his love to her on a daily basis just write a letter and never look back. He was so clean about it that she was never able to put the puzzle together. He made things so comfortable that she couldn't even question in court what was being offered. He gave her everything free and clear. Every month the money rolled in and there was more than enough to meet all of their needs at the level they were used to living. No wants. She could have continued to stay home and take care of the girls; but too much time and too many questions would have destroyed her mind quickly.

So she chose to become a working mom; to step out into the work force and brush up her skills. Which if she were honest with herself, were rusty to say the least. Technology had moved on in 20 years and she had to do some catching up. But she had friends who were more than willing to give her that chance and she determined to rise to the occasion. And she did. In just a few months she had taken a job as a secretary to the Dean of Students at the University. Michael Dunn had been a friend of Gale's for years. He probably felt like he had to help in whatever way that he could. Genie didn't need his pity. She was worth everything that she was paid. She worked hard; took evening classes to brush up on any skills that she was lacking and she brought to the office an enthusiasm that brightened everyone's day. Obviously she was a great actress. No one knew how broken she was inside.

One evening when waiting for a meeting to start, Michael asked her how she was handling the loss in her home? She thought that was a unique way to ask the question; although, as she thought about it, it really was a loss. There was a piece gone that no one could find. That piece wasn't coming back.

"How do you do it? You are always so happy and make us all feel better no matter what the circumstance. Don't you ever just want to scream and cry? I mean…what happened? Even those of us who considered Gale a best friend didn't see this coming. We don't understand. Do you?" Michael asked.

"Michael," I said, "I can't change anything that happened. Gale left us with no way to get answers to our questions. He was clean, neat and professional. I will never understand. But, I have three beautiful girls who deserve a chance at whatever normal looks like from that moment on. So everyday I get up and do the best that I can to make sure that happens in their world. I learned that I can't control anything. I can only be responsible for me and the job that I have been given to do. The girls are my focus." I smiled as if everything in my world was right side up.

"Michael, I know the risk that you took in hiring me. It could have been disastrous. Here I was a broken wife of a friend who wasn't who we all thought that he was. You had to be unsure about the decision to open up your office and the students of this campus to me. To put me into a position that required someone who was quick thinking, enthusiastic and able to balance multi-plates at once; it was a risk on your part. I will always be grateful for the opportunity that you have given me. And I promise that with all of my ability I will never intentionally let you down.

Michael laughed, "When I saw your resume′ come across my desk, I didn't think twice. You have all of the skills that my students need. For years I have watched you entertain the most prominent people of wealth. Yet you can be with someone who has nothing and make him or her feel there is no one more special on earth. You have always balanced schedules and multi-tasked to get the jobs done that no one else in the community would ever volunteer for. You are gentle and yet firm. No one would ever say that you were a push over. Yet I have seen you comfort a broken student who wasn't sure that they could do one more day. I have watched as they have left with a renewed strength. It was my pleasure to offer you the position that you have so completely filled." Michael finished by adding, "Gale must have been out of his mind to leave a complete package like you".

And that was the last time that we ever talked about my situation or Gale. We put that white elephant to rest that evening and continued a working relationship that has been beneficial to both of us. My needs are met on a day to day basis. My time is filled and I don't have too many hours to think. The girls are my importance and life goes on.

But…in the nights when I lay in my bedroom by myself, alone and desperate, there is no one that can comfort me. I cry and I ask why? The answer never comes. There is no way to understand. There is no one to feel my pain. There is no Gale to plan our future with or laugh about something that the girls said or did. Many nights sleep eludes me and when it does come, it is from the exhaustion of crying.

Then morning dawns and I jump out of bed determined that today, while the sun shines, I will be joyful. Today I will be all that I am supposed to be. Today I will fix problems, answer questions, and smile as if I don't have a concern in the world. Today I will go home after work and have a wonderful meal with my daughters. We will talk and be as normal as possible. I will tuck them into bed even though they are grown and don't need me. But, I need them. Because when I leave their rooms, I will have to go back to my room and try to get through another night.

CHAPTER 7

PSALM 139:23-24
Search me, O God, and know my heart,
test me and know my anxious thoughts.
See if there is any offensive way in me,
and lead me in the way everlasting.

WHO AM I

NOELLE WAS TAKEN BY THE BEAUTY SURROUNDING THE home that Brad and his mother live in. The house, a two-story ranch with a huge porch that circled three sides, was nestled in the beauty of trees with a small creek that was flowing around the house from the back and through the front yard. It disappeared into the woods that surrounded their home. Bird houses were everywhere and the trees that had already turned colors created a majestic picture. The maple leaves danced in reds, yellows, and bright oranges. Probably because of so much rain, there was a carpeting of leaves already lying on the ground. Noelle could almost feel how wonderful the leaves would be on her bare feet if she could have taken off her shoes and marched carelessly across the soft silk of the beauty that was laid out before her.

There was more. As Brad held the door of the truck open for her, she stepped out into a feeling of peace. The sounds of the rain falling lightly through the leaves created a symphony of music that tickled her ears. She smiled at Brad. She couldn't help it.

"It's beautiful here. You and your family must be very happy." Noelle said.

"It is beautiful. And as a family we have worked very hard to make it a place where people feel comfortable and want to stop and stay awhile. Mom is never happier than when all of those porch rockers are filled up with people and she is serving one of her special deserts.

"Come on and let's get you into the house and out of the rain. I'll grab your suitcase if you would like?"

"Thank you again for being so nice. I really do appreciate all that you're doing. I know that you must have had plans for your day. I'm sorry." Noelle answered.

"No problem. If we can't help someone in need then what good are we to His kingdom?"

Brad's reply took her somewhat by surprise. She had to think a minute about what he meant. Then it dawned on her that he must have been talking about being a good person and God and all that. Well Brad certainly had done his best to practice the 'What Would Jesus Do' stuff today. She had seen the bracelets on some of the kids at school.

Brad ushered her into a home that was softly decorated and instantly she could feel the atmosphere of warmth. The rooms were very open and inviting. At the end of the room was a large fireplace with some kind of an insert that glowed with a cozy fire. She couldn't help but think how nice it would be to cuddle up in front of that fire with a blanket, a cup of tea and a great book. The lighting was dim and soft music was playing somewhere through speakers that could be heard all around. She felt like she had just walked into a movie set. To the back of the house was a huge kitchen with a snack bar that circled almost all of the room. Lots of sturdy wooden backed high chairs were pushed up to the bar. It looked like a lot of food and good times happened around that bar. There was a sitting room filled with comfy overstuffed chairs. The wall had an old looking cross with a purple cloth draped across it. There was writing surrounded it that said, “He did this for you and for me. John 3:16.” She noticed candles were everywhere. It gave such a homey feel to every room. To the right of the kitchen was the largest dining room table that she had ever seen.

Brad noticed her looking at the table and he laughed. “I told you that my mom loves to cook. The more who show up the better she likes it. You would think after cooking for the whole town every day she would get tired of that. Not mom. She was born to cook.”

“Why don’t I show you to one of the guest rooms and you can get that shower that I promised you. While you’re getting cleaned up I’ll make the call on your tire and make sure that we get that ordered before the end of the day. Do you want to follow me?”

Noelle, nodding, followed him to the back side of the kitchen and up the stairs. The second floor was just as welcoming as the first. Flowers and candles adorned the tables that were set about by chairs that were just there to rest and read in.

Brad walked her to the end of the hall and he opened a door and stood back to allow her to enter. The room was breath taking. There on the center wall was a beautiful poster bed. It was done in soft yellows and country blues with homemade quilts and pillows on the bed. There was a matching window quilt on a huge window and she was eager to see the view behind it. Just past the bed was another door that led into a full bathroom with a huge tub that was calling to her. There was a spicy smell to both rooms. Not over powering; earthy and peaceful. If she had not been so tired, she would have giggled in anticipation of running a large bath and soaking the sorrow of the last three days away. She turned and smiled her gratitude again.

"I'll leave your case on this bench. There is a lock on both of these doors. You are perfectly safe. I'm going down stairs to use the phone and then I have a few chores that are calling to me out in the barn. You make yourself at home. If you find that you're still hungry, my mom would be upset if you didn't just get in that refrigerator and find something that would take that craving away. I'll check on you when I get done outside. But take your time. It'll probably take me a couple of hours. The house belongs to you for awhile. My mom will be working late at the restaurant and this is my brother's night of late classes at the college. There is no one to disturb you. Relax, soak, and sleep. You look like you could use some quiet time. I'll see you when I get back in."

She walked with Brad to the door and smiled. "Again, I don't know what to say. I can't thank you enough for all of your kindness."

"Take care of yourself. That's all the thanks that I need." He turned to leave as she closed and locked the door.

"God help her to find the peace that surpasses all understanding. Give her the peace that only You can give. I am leaving her in Your hands Father. Send Your angels to minister to her. She needs You. Amen.

Noelle opened her case and found a pair of fleece pants and a sweatshirt. She was eager to wash away the grime of the last three days.

As she stood in the shower with the water running over her face, she puzzled at the direction that the last few hours had taken. Never had she imagined any of this. She washed her hair and allowed her thoughts to roam into tomorrow when her mom and sisters would be home. She could only imagine the pain that they would feel. If she could have saved them from that, she would have. But she couldn't. She did not have any better choices. She was working this out moment by moment. She could not see tomorrow.

After showering, she could not resist the welcoming call of the tub. She plugged the drain and sunk down into what felt like pure, warm silk. She ran the tub full of water and laid there letting the warmth ease her tense muscles. What would her mom do when she found the letter? Would she call Noelle's friends first? What about the police? Would they report her missing? As the warmth engulfed her, she dozed until the water cooled and woke her up. Startling it took her a moment to realize where she was. Getting out of the tub she wrapped in a fluffy towel, combed and dried her hair and rubbed oil into her eyes. Thank goodness for the eye drops that she had. The drops soothed her dry eyes. Then looking into the mirror, she wondered, "Who am I?" The person looking back was someone totally different from a few weeks ago. Where did that person go?

Noelle scolded herself. Do not think any more today. The morning will bring with it new questions. For tonight just shut down and relax. Tomorrow you will be able to think better.

That decision being made she straightened the rooms and decided to go back to that fire and couch that was calling to her from the time that she had walked into the house. She closed the door and walked quietly down the stairs.

Brad must have already used the phone and was gone to the barn. There was a blanket on the back of the couch and wrapping it around her; she curled up into the corner. The couch was welcoming and so was the crackle of the fire. Watching the sparks behind the glass doors was mesmerizing and shortly Noelle was sleeping peacefully. The sorrow of the previous days had been replaced by protective hands. Her last thoughts before drifting off were of those strong hands. The hands of Brad Conroy.

CHAPTER 8

PSALM 42:8-11
By day the LORD directs His love,
at night His song is with me—a
prayer to the God of my life.
I say to God my Rock
"Why have You forgotten me? Why must I go about mourning,
oppressed by the enemy?"
My bones suffer mortal agony as my foes taunt me,
Saying to me all day long,
"Where is Your God?"
Why are you downcast, O my soul?
Why so disturbed within me?
Put your hope in God, for I will yet praise Him,
my Savior and my God.

OFFERING DIRECTION

BRAD FINISHED HIS CHORES IN RECORD TIME. HIS THOUGHTS were constantly drifting back to the girl in the house. Who was she? What was her name? What was her story? Over and over he asked God for direction on how to proceed. He knew that she was fragile. He didn't understand why; but, for some reason he wanted to have all of the answers.

As the rain continued to fall, Brad headed to the house. There was an excitement building inside of him that was very unusual and much unexpected. Yet he welcomed it with every fiber of his being.

Not sure what he would find, he entered the house quietly. He opened the door to the utility room and took off his barn coat. Leaving the barn shoes in that back room, he went into his bedroom which was off of the entry room and showered and changed into jeans and a clean white, button shirt. Feeling more presentable, he continued quietly walking through the kitchen and into the main living room of the house.

What greeted him was a vision that took his breath away. Cuddled up on the couch in a little ball, wrapped tightly in a blanket, with the fire glowing beyond her was the most beautiful picture of someone between child and woman that he had ever seen. He stood paralyzed as he watched the silkiness of her hair move in response to the smooth, flow of her breathing. Her hair fell in a mixture of curls and waves around her face framing her features ever so gently.

He sat in the chair across from her and as he watched, he began to feel like an intruder invading the peaceful quiet that encompassed her rest. He would guess her to be younger than he originally thought. No more than 18 years he would surmise. Her eyes, though less swelled than before, still held the tell tale signs of hours of tears falling from them.

He wondered about her past. What would her future hold? Was there more sorrow in store for her? Could he do something that could buffer the pain that was to come? And why did he feel so strongly that she was headed in the wrong direction? Was that a nudge from God? There were so many questions floating around in his mind.

Noelle began to surface from the drowsy depth of sleep. She could feel his eyes on her as she slowly opened hers. She could see that he was deep in thought and she broke the silence.

"Are you done with what you had to do?"

"Yes. Yes. I'm done." Brad didn't tell her that he had worked faster than usual so that he could get back into the house to check on her. "You look like you had a little rest. Are you feeling better?" Brad questioned.

Noelle slowly stretched and set up. "I had a wonderful soak in the tub and then I couldn't resist the draw of this cozy corner. I think that I must have drifted off to sleep as soon as I curled up in this blanket and began to watch the fire spark."

"When I come in from the barn, I like a cup of coffee and a good book in front of that fire." He thought to himself that her company would beat a good book any day. Surprised, he wondered where those thoughts were coming from.

Perhaps he needed to move around a bit and focus on something else. "How would you like me to make us some hot tea or cocoa?"

She stretched again and with a big smile said, "Hot chocolate would be wonderful…if that wouldn't cause you too much trouble?"

"No trouble at all. I'll be right back." Brad went into the kitchen and busied himself with the task at hand.

From the kitchen she heard him say, "I checked on your car before I came in and everything looks fine. Not that I would expect anything different. We don't usually get a lot of traffic down these roads, especially late at night."

"Thank you", Noelle twisted so that she could see him at work in the kitchen. "That's so kind of you to go out of your way to reassure me. I'm sorry that I've caused you so much added trouble. I promise that I'll make it up to you."

"It hasn't been any trouble at all. Really it's fine. I talked with the station and they'll have your tire in sometime tomorrow in the afternoon. They don't stock a lot of different sizes. They're a small station. If you needed more than they could do for you, it would be a trip of about 50 miles farther down the main highway. I thought that in the afternoon, we could go into town with your wheel and they can make the switch. Maybe we could have lunch at my mom's restaurant."

Noelle thought that sounded nice. She wondered why the idea of spending time with this man would bring thoughts of peace in the middle of her mess.

She just answered quietly, "That would be very nice, thank you".

Brad carried the steaming cups into the living room and handed the cocoa to Noelle before he sat back down in the chair he had left earlier. There was a comfortable silence between them as they watched the crackling fire and sipped their drinks.

Noelle broke into the quiet, "When do you think that your mom will be home? I hope that she won't feel like I've inconvenienced her; especially after a long day at work. I wouldn't want to cause her any more trouble."

"Actually, I talked with her about an hour ago and she thought that she would be leaving pretty quickly. So I would expect to see her anytime. You'll like my mom; but don't let her intimidate you. I learned along time ago that behind that rough facade beats a heart as big as Texas. She has a love for everyone. She wants to help fix all of their problems. I guess that's where I get it from. She's a wise woman and I try to always listen and take her advice. She hasn't stirred me wrong. In fact, she has saved me a lot of heartache over the years. Just be ready to answer questions. Plus, she talks fast.

Just as he finished talking the head lights crested the window and Brad said, "There she is now. I'll go out and see if she has anything that needs to be carried. I'll be right back." With that said Brad got up, put his cup down on the kitchen bar, and walked out through the door. She was left alone waiting in anticipation and worry. Questions? She wasn't up to questions. She hadn't put together her plan yet. She didn't have a story prepared. What was she going to say? She didn't want to say too much. And she certainly didn't want to say anything that would give away any information that would help anyone find her. She would have to be careful how she answered. She would have to guard her words.

While Brad was out with his mom, Noelle stood and fluffed the couch. She quickly folded up the blanket and put it back in the place that she had first found it. She did not want this woman to find her lounging. Noelle would not want her to think that she was without manners. Her mom would have been appalled. Noelle would face her standing and she would politely introduce herself. She would direct this conversation on her own terms.

CHAPTER 9

PSALM 25:1-5
To You, O LORD, I lift up my soul;
in You I trust, O my God.
Do not let me be put to shame,
nor let my enemies triumph over me.
No one whose hope is in You will ever be put to shame,
but they will be put to shame
who are treacherous without excuse.
Show me Your ways, O LORD, teach me Your paths;
guide me in Your truth and teach me,
for You are God my Savior,
and my hope is in You all day long.

GETTING TO THE BOTTOM

BRAD'S DESCRIPTION OF HIS MOTHER WAS MORE THAN ACcurate. The kitchen door opened and into the room blew whirl wind of a woman. Not more than five foot tall, long hair pulled back in a pony tail, Noelle was amazed at the speed that she moved. Guessing her to be in her fifties, she moved with the agility of someone much younger. She couldn't have weighed much over 100 pounds. She was barking orders as fast as Brad could move. There was food for the refrigerator, food for the freezer, potatoes to go to the cellar and empty jars for the basement.

When the commotion of the entrance was done and everything was in its place, Mrs. Conroy turned her attention to Noelle. She came and sat down on the couch and patted the spot right next to her. Noelle sat down. The woman smiled a very similar smile, dimples, and all, to the smile that had flashed across Brad's face all day.

"My! Aren't you a pretty thing?" Brad's mom offered her hand and said, "I'm Angelina and you are?"

Noelle hesitated only a moment and said, "My name is Noelle, Noelle Smith. It's so kind of you to offer me a room in your home. Brad has been so helpful with my car." There was something about this woman that required the truth that she hadn't intended to give; she just couldn't help it.

"Well you just make yourself comfortable. The Lord didn't give us this big home to just sit in. You are more than welcome to stay as long as you need to. Now…tell me your story. What is a youngster like you doing out in this big old world by yourself? Where are you headed? Where did you come from? Who knows where you are? Have you let your folks know that you are okay?" Angelina questioned.

Noelle didn't know how to answer. She started and then stopped. She could feel her face turning red and the tears were welling up. She couldn't cry. Angelina would know that something was wrong. Breathe deep, she instructed herself and she counted the breaths as they came. She was almost to ten when Angelina wrapped her arms around her and began to talk in soothing sounds.

"There, there little one," she said. "It's going to be all right. You tell me all about it. We'll find a way to make it all work."

Noelle fell into her arms. It felt so good to have someone hold her and reassure her that there was a way to make everything work out. She already missed her mother so much.

Angelina looked towards the kitchen at Brad. "Bradley, I think that I heard some commotion in the barn when I was outside, why don't you go take a look. Noelle and I have some girl talking to do."

"Sure bet!" Brad answered as he headed for the door feeling embarrassed; as if he was intruding on a private conversation. Noelle. As he headed to the barn, he mulled the name over in his mind. He liked the way it rolled off his tongue. Perfect name for someone so pretty.

Hearing the door close, Angelina continued, "Now that we are alone, you feel free to unload on me. I won't promise you that I will agree; but I will promise to listen."

She soothed Noelle's hair as she was talking and the motion had such a calming effect that Noelle could feel her head, almost on its own volition, slowly lower and rest on Angelina's shoulder.

The tears began to fall and Noelle said, "There are only my mom and two sisters, whom I love very much. I screwed things up and I couldn't let them suffer because of my mistakes...so I decided to leave. I wrote them a letter and while they were visiting my aunt, I packed up and left. I didn't know what else to do. I'm so ashamed with the decisions that I've made and I'm going to take care of things by myself. No one else should have to pay the consequences for choices that I've made. That just wouldn't be fair."

"Okay", Angelina started, "I'm going to ask a few questions that any mother would need to know.

"How long have you been gone?"

"Three days, but they don't know yet; my mom and the girls won't be home until tomorrow." Noelle answered.

"When she gets home, will she be able to get a hold of you. I'm sure you know how important it is for a mom to know that her little chicks are safe."

"I left my phone there so that no one could track me. I'm sure that she's been calling to check on me and is assuming that I've lost my phone again...I sometimes do that."

Angelina frowned, "You know that isn't going to work for her. She'll be worried sick and that certainly is 'her having to deal with a bad choice on your part.'" She winked at me. "We'll have to find a way to fix that decision."

Feeling myself being pulled away from the warmth of her embrace, Angelina looked me straight in the eyes and said, "I'm going to take a wild guess and say that the reason that you are in this situation is because you're pregnant…correct?"

The question took Noelle by surprise. Pausing, she answered slowly, "Yes. I hadn't told anyone. I haven't even said the words out loud. It sounds so foreign to me." Noelle looked at the ground as the shame hit like an ocean wave. She started to cry again. "I was a good girl. It shouldn't have happened to me. I didn't do things like that."

"Do you think that only bad girls get themselves into circumstances that they can't control? We live in a fallen world and the forces of evil advance daily. There is a kingdom at work here that loves to see lives destroyed; but I'm here to tell you… that only happens if we allow him to win. And I am talking about satan. Now for me…I get up every morning and I determine, and I say that assuredly because it is a choice that I make, I determine that satan is going to know that I'm awake and that I'm going to do everything I can to disturb the forces of Hell. You're going to have to make a decision. You're at a crossroads. Either you can choose to let him win or you can find a way to kick his butt.

I felt her finger below my chin as she pulled my face to eye level.

"I know that the decisions that are to be made are not easy ones. I know that personally. Someday I'll tell you the whole story. For tonight just know that I was in the same shoes that you are in and I had to make a choice too. I didn't have anybody telling me there were options. I live every day with the knowledge of what my decision did. I know how lonely you're feeling. I can tell you, beyond a shadow of a doubt, that you are not alone. You have a Heavenly Father who knew this day would come; He knew that this baby would happen and He already has a plan for the life of your unborn child. The decisions that you make will either allow for God's plan to be fulfilled or it will end the future that this child was created for."

I looked into the kindest face that I have ever seen. She did know how I was feeling. She understood. I could almost feel her pain mingle with mine. But what did all of that plan and purpose stuff mean? Noelle was confused about that.

"Tomorrow will be another day for that discussion. This is too heavy a conversation to have before closing your eyes to sleep. I want you to go up and get ready for bed. I'm going to get you another glass of hot chocolate and I'll bring it to your room and say good night." Angelina hugged me close one more time and stood with her hands stretched out.

I took a hold of those hands as if they were a life preserver and I was drowning. She turned me toward the stairs and sent me on my way.

As I washed my face, I walked back through all that had happened to me. I had never really thought of God as personal and active in my life on a daily basis; however today certainly caused me to pause. As I looked back, I could see a definite leading; even in the small details.

I climbed into bed and heard a soft knock on the door.

"Come in."

Angelina entered carrying a tray with an assortment. As she set it down on the bedside table she handed me the cup of warm chocolate. "Now drink this and here are a few cookies to go with it. I wasn't sure how the mornings are for you, so here are some packages of crackers. I always found that if I ate some crackers before getting out of bed my stomach seemed to work better for me. If you need anything else, you just make yourself at home. I'll be here when you wake up in the morning and we can talk some more then.

She hugged me one more time and turned to leave.

"Angelina, thank you so much…for everything. You and your son have both been kind…beyond measure. I'll never be able to tell you how much it's meant to me. I haven't talked to anyone about…well…you know. It's been so lonely.

"I know Honey…I really do know. Now sleep tight.

And on that she closed the door and turned off the light. I was left alone with the quiet of the night. It only seemed appropriate to pray.

God, if You're listening, thank you for sending me this way. I don't understand it all. I'm confused about why You would direct my life now and not before; You know before that night. But, please don't stop. I mean don't leave me alone to walk on my own. It's a terrible place to be on your own. I need You; and I don't even know what that means. Help me to make the right decisions. I haven't been doing so well on my own. Thank You. Amen. Oh...plus will You watch over my mom and sisters tomorrow and help them to not be too sad. Good night.

Noelle sipped her hot chocolate in the quiet of the dark bedroom until it was gone. She wondered what tomorrow would bring. As she put down her coffee cup and snuggled into the bed, she pulled the covers over her head and was fast asleep.

CHAPTER 10

PSALM 143:4-10
The enemy pursues me; he crushes me to the ground;
He makes me dwell in darkness like those long dead.
So my spirit grows faint within me;
My heart with me is dismayed.
I remember the day of long ago;
I meditate on all Your works
And consider what Your hands have done.
I spread out my hands to You; my soul thirsts for You like a parched land. Selah
Answer me quickly, O LORD; my spirit falls.
Do not hide Your face from me or
I will be like those who go down to the pit.
Let the morning bring me word of your unfailing love,
For I have put my trust in You.
Show me the way I should go, for to You I lift my soul.
Rescue me from my enemies, O LORD,
For I hide myself in You.
Teach me to do Your will, for You are my God;
May Your good Spirit lead me on level ground.

WHEN YOU NEED A PLACE TO HIDE

BRADLEY HAD PUTTERED AROUND IN THE BARN GIVING THE women plenty of time to talk. He didn't want to get in the way of an important conversation. He knew his mom well enough to know that she would get to the bottom of this quicker than anyone. Plus, there were always things to do out here. The work was never all done. That was okay with him. He also knew that someday the farm would be his. His younger brother had already made it clear that the sooner he was off the farm the better that he'd like it.

Eyan, almost two years younger than himself, was never content. He was always looking for an adventure. That was the difference between them. Brad loved the consistency of everyday life on the farm and Eyan had a love for the Lord that was going to take him to other places. He had a passion to reach the lost. His mission was to find those who hadn't heard about Jesus and tell them He loves them. As the older brother, he saw opportunity to live out his love for the Lord in the everyday life around him. Their differences only drew them closer. They were as bonded as brothers could be. Their parents had made sure that they knew the importance of family. The example had been set for them…God first, family next and then self.

Brad's mind wandered through so many memories as he swept and cleaned up the barn floors. He smiled to himself as he thought about the many hours that he and Eyan had spent shooting hoops in the loft with Dad. He could almost hear the laughter as the games heated up. In the winter you could see your breath; yet you were never cold. The heat from the cows always warmed the air. Now most of the cows were gone and so was Dad.

It was sudden. No one had expected it. Dad had always been so active. He was never sick. "Bradley", he would say, "If you would get more fresh air you wouldn't have that cold. Fresh air kills all of the bugs. Look at me…the picture of health." Then there was that day when Brad and Eyan went out to the barn to do chores after school and found him on the floor. Just like that he was gone; bad heart valve; happened fast; did not suffer. Those were the words of encouragement that they were told. As if those words would make them feel better. What did comfort them was that Dad was a believer who talked about his faith daily.

"You never know how many days the Lord has planned for you, so make the best of everyone of them," he would say. And he did. He also made sure that the legacy that he left behind was one of love; love for Jesus, love for each other and a love for a reunion one day in heaven where we would all be together again.

Mom, Eyan and I try everyday to make sure that we carry ourselves in such a way that Dad would be proud of us. He taught us whom our strength comes from. Our strength comes from the Lord. He taught us how to stand firm on the Rock, Jesus Christ, and not be tossed like a wave on the sea. He taught us the great commission to go out and make disciples. But most importantly, he taught us to love our fellow man as ourselves.

These were good things for a father to teach his family and they have served us well. Tonight because of who he taught us to be, there is a sad little woman child in our house and I hope that before she moves on we'll be able to show her that life is never hopeless. Every time the sun comes up is a new chance for a better life.

"Bradley." Mom broke through my deep thoughts as she entered the barn. "Come here and sit with me on this hay and let's talk."

Just as she began, Eyan walked into the barn.

"What's up? Why's everyone out here. House to cozy for you guys tonight?"

"Hi Honey," Mom said. "I'm glad you're here. I was just getting ready to have a heart to heart talk with your brother. Now I'll only have to go through this once. I want to share something from my past with the two of you."

Turning to Eyan she said, "To bring you up to speed, there is a young woman in our home in the guest room. Brad found her down the road in a car with a flat tire. She needed a new tire so that's been taken care of and will be at the station tomorrow. But, she is in need of something else. That something else is causing this conversation that I'm about to have with you boys. It isn't something that I'm comfortable with; but, I think that it's necessary to help this girl. I didn't want to share something with her that the two of you didn't know."

She certainly had caught our attention. I watched as my mom's face showed the pain that I knew was in her heart for this girl. "Mom, you tell us whatever you want us to know. We won't share anything that you say." Eyan placed his arm around his mother's shoulders and gave her a comforting squeeze.

"I know. This is not about what you might share. This is about what I'm going to share with you." She said.

With a momentary pause, she continued. "I'm going to tell you something that no one around here knows. Only your father was privy to what I'm about to say. But, I'm going to tell you because I think that it's something that I'm going to have to share with this broken young lady. Perhaps in telling her my story I can keep her from making the same mistake that I made; a mistake that could torture her for a lifetime."

"Okay. You tell us whatever you need to." I said. Eyan nodded his agreement with me.

"You know that I wasn't from this town. I grew up about 100 miles from here. I met your dad at a church camp where we were both counselors for the summer. We had been out of high school for two years. We fell in love over time and your dad thought that we had built our love based on truth and trust and a love for the Lord."

We could see that whatever Mom was going to say made her very uncomfortable.

"When your dad asked me to marry him, I knew that I was the luckiest girl in the whole world. I loved him deeply. He was my knight in shining armor. But, I told him no."

"Why?" Eyan and I asked at the same time.

"I didn't think that I was good enough for him. He deserved more than what I had to offer." Mom replied.

"Obviously Dad didn't agree." Eyan said.

"No…and he wouldn't take no for an answer. You know how your dad was when he had his mind set on something." She laughed and continued. "Everyday for weeks, he would call me and ask the same question, "Have you decided that you can't live without me yet?"

"Finally one day I agreed to meet him at the park for a picnic lunch. He was relentless. I broke; I started pouring the whole story out to him. He was speechless until I was done."

"Then he looked at me and said, 'If Jesus doesn't see you anyway but spotless and perfect, then why should I see you any differently? If Jesus is coming back for you as His bride, why can't I have you as my bride while we are on this earth?'"

"I loved your dad more at that moment then I thought humanly possible. Our love only grew from then on."

"He told me that day in the park that if I ever wanted to talk about it again, he was there for me. But, if I didn't, that was okay too. We never spoke about it again and he never treated me any differently from that day forward. He really knew how to exhibit the true love of Christ."

"Mom, I don't know how Brad feels about this; but speaking for myself, if it was good enough for Dad, then it's good enough for me. Don't feel like you have to share something that personal with us. If you need to share it with the girl in the house, then that's between you and her. Sharing isn't going to change the way that we feel about you. If sharing will help her and her walk with Christ, then okay. I don't see what that has to do with us; unless you just need to talk about it now." Eyan finished.

Brad watched as his mother's eyes welled up and a lone tear slowly fell down the curve of her cheek. He reached up and wiping the tear away said, "Mom, Dad loved you enough to understand the prize that he was getting. He always taught us that our sins are 'as far as the east is from the west' when we confess them to God; to God Mom, not to us. You do whatever you feel God is telling you to do. Don't worry about us. We're a family and that's never going to change from here to eternity.

Mom threw open her arms wide and said, "Bradley, Eyan, you are the best sons that a crazy mom could ever have."

We held that family hug long enough for Mom to pull her emotions back into check and then she smacked each of our cheeks.

"Let's go to bed. I have a feeling that tomorrow is going to be a long day."

As we walked together into the house, I couldn't help but feel that Dad would have been proud of his boys tonight.

Eyan caught up with me in the kitchen before going to bed. "Dude, what's up with all the drama here tonight?"

"Wait till you meet this girl." I said.

"Well for starters, does she have a name?" Eyan asked.

"Yup! Noelle…her name is Noelle." I couldn't help but grin when I said her name. Just the thought of her made me smile.

Eyan gave me a look that only a brother could give. He smiled. More like a sheepish grin. You know the one that says he just figured out the secret. "Well…I can't wait to see what the morning brings. This should be interesting. See you then."

"What?" I asked oblivious to his thoughts.

"Oh…nothing. Have sweet dreams Bro." He smirked as he snapped me with the towel from his shoulders and headed to his bedroom.

I followed turning off all of the lights on my way. Getting into bed, I prayed, Lord, thank you for this day and the family that you've given me. Help Mom to sleep well and not worry.

Let tomorrow bring what it will. But in all things with prayer and supplication; Your will be done. Amen.

CHAPTER 10

PSALM 23:1-4
The LORD is my shepherd, I shall not be in want.
He makes me lie down in green pastures,
He leads me beside quiet waters,
He restores my soul.
He guides me in paths of righteousness
for His name's sake.
Even though I walk through the valley
of the shadow of death,
I will fear no evil, for You are with me;
Your rod and Your staff they comfort me.

A MISSED LIFE

THE SUN PEEKED ITS WAY THROUGH THE WINDOW AND BEGAN to shine on Noelle's face. She slowly opened her eyes. The newness of the room that she was in confused her at first and then the memory of the last few days slowly began to resurface from the recesses of her sleep filled mind.

She stretched and yawned and wanted to snuggle back under the covers and into the bed that allowed her to sleep so soundly. There had been no dreams to disturb the much needed rest, just the sweet sleep of a peaceful night.

To soon though, reality began to creep back into her thoughts and she sat up quickly looking for a clock. Shock set in as she saw that the clock said 10:00 a.m. She must have slept twelve hours. As she jumped out of bed, her stomach did a flip and reminded her that it had been a long time since she had last put anything into it. She remembered the tray of crackers that Angelina had brought to her last night and reached for a package. Sitting on the edge of the bed she opened one and nibbled slowly. The salty taste was welcomed and as she swallowed one bite after another the internal rumblings began to subside.

The morning sickness had been tolerable so far. Or maybe she had just ignored it. If she had surrendered to those feelings, it would have been harder to hide the facts from her family. But here, where no one knew her, it just seemed easier. Last night proved that as she looked back. She had confessed the unspeakable to a total stranger.

Angelina! What must she be thinking? Here she is being so kind and I'm just lazing around for hours. At that thought, Noelle finished the crackers, washed up, got dressed, and quickly headed down the stairs into the kitchen.

Wonderful smells greeted her as she rounded the bend in the stairs. She could smell eggs and sausage mixed with a strong, nutty coffee aroma. Her mouth began to water.

As she stepped into the room, there was Angelina taking fresh baked bread out of the oven. The smell was almost more than she could stand.

"Good morning." Noelle spoke softly in a hesitant voice.

"Well, good morning to you." Angelina's smiling face beamed at her. "You must be hungry. I have breakfast ready for you. Come and sit at the bar so that we can talk while I fix your plate."

"Thank you, it smells wonderful. But, I feel so bad that you went to so much trouble. I know that Brad said you were so busy at the restaurant. You certainly didn't need an extra mouth to feed here at your home."

"Nonsense! This is what I do. I feed mouths all day and I do it because it brings me joy to serve others. Today I just get to do that in my own home, for awhile anyway. At some point I'll have to go into the restaurant. But for now, if it's okay with you, we're going to spend some time together." Angelina offered such a loving smile that no one could have refused her.

"I don't know what to say. You've been so kind to me. How will I ever repay you?" I could feel the tears starting to fill my eyes.

"Now don't start that. I think that you've cried all of the tears that you can afford to cry for awhile. Your well is going to dry up." She offered me a plate of the most wonderful looking food and said, "eat…that's thanks enough."

Pouring me a glass of orange juice, and sitting down beside me with a slice of hot bread, she sipped her coffee quietly and watched as I ate. I could tell that something was weighing on her and I hoped that something was not me.

When we had both finished eating she looked at me sadly and said, "I want to tell you a story. It isn't a very nice story. But, it's a story that needs to be told today. There was a young girl. She was your age and she grew up in a loving family who taught her right from wrong. When she graduated, she couldn't wait to be out on her own so that she could make her own choices in life. She met a boy. He swept her off her feet. He was handsome and funny. And he represented all of the things that the girl had been told her whole life to avoid. Only now she didn't have to. She could do whatever she wanted. And she did.

At this Angelina paused and she stared into her coffee cup. She was quiet for moments as if she were struggling to remember something that she had forgotten or tucked far away.

Noelle could see that this was very uncomfortable for her to tell. "You don't have to tell me this."

As if she had been pulled back from somewhere far away, she patted Noelle's hand and said, "I know that I don't have to. I'm choosing to tell you this."

She continued, "You can only tempt fate so many times before you get caught. I got caught. I was that girl and one day I found myself pregnant. The only place that I thought I could go for help was to the boy that had played a part in the creating of the problem. Unfortunately, he didn't want to hear about it. According to him, this wasn't his problem. He made it clear that this was my problem."

"He said, 'If you need money, I can come up with half of the cost to get rid of this.'"

"I said, 'No thanks, I can get rid of the problem for nothing by just walking away from you.'"

"And I did. So now I was pregnant and totally alone."

There was another long pause while she gathered her thoughts before continuing.

"You see, I had seen what happened to girls who find themselves in these situations. I grew up in small town USA in a strict church and they were not kind. In fact the girls and their families were ostracized. They were treated like second class citizens. I knew that I couldn't put my family through that. They hadn't done anything wrong."

"So, I made an appointment. First I had to meet with a lady and she told me about the procedure and how there was nothing to it. She emphasized how this was nothing more than a mass of cells. She told me that life had not even begun yet. I was told that it was safer at this point to have this procedure done then it was to carry a pregnancy to full term. I agreed to sign the papers and made an appointment for the next day."

"I drove myself there crying so hard I could barely see the road. I reminded myself that this was for my family. I was protecting them. I made myself believe that there was no baby yet. After all it was just a mass of cells. If it was a baby, I wouldn't do it. But....it wasn't a baby. All the material said that it wouldn't be a baby for another month. Just a mass of cells. I repeated that over and over. Just a mass of cells. Not really a life yet. Just a mass of cells."

Angelina took a deep breath as if she was looking for the

strength to continue. I could see the tears welling up in her eyes. She sniffed. I reached over and took her hand.

She squeezed my hand and continued, “I walked into that clinic. The smell of antiseptic and bleach hit me full force. I kept thinking that they were just going to clean this problem away. Nice and tidy. No one had to know. Right? The problem would just go away and I would go on with my plans. Only I would make better choices. This would be like a fresh start. After all isn’t that what God would want me to do? I had always heard that He was the God of fresh starts.”

“I was told to sit in a waiting room. I couldn’t stop crying. The lady who was already waiting told me, ‘It isn’t so bad and it’ll be over before you know it.’”

“I asked, ‘Have you been here before?’”

“The lady said, ‘Oh yah. You get used to it.’”

“I knew, beyond a shadow of a doubt, that I would never find myself in this place again.”

“A lady dressed like a nurse came to the room and called my name. She smiled at me and asked me to follow her. I stood; but I wasn’t sure that my legs would carry me. She turned back and took my arm. She helped me to another room where she instructed me about what to do with my clothes and said that she would be right back.”

“I did as I was told. I put on the gown and I folded my clothes. I remembered seeing the tears falling on my shirt and it was getting wet. I just couldn’t stop crying.”

Angelina got up and got a box of tissues. We were both sobbing so hard. I could feel the fear of the young Angelina and I knew the sorrow that had brought her to that point. Her pain was real and I could understand the feeling of hopelessness.

She blew her nose, “The nurse lady returned and asked me questions about what I’d been told the day before at the required initial appointment. She asked me if I was making this decision on my own accord. I had to sign a paper saying that no one was making me do this. I signed…because no one was making me do this. I did this on my own. I made the decision because it was just a mass of cells."

"I was taken to a room that looked like an operating room. There were machines. They had me get on the table and they set everything up."

"In came a doctor. He said, 'this will only take a short time and now you'll feel a little stinging.'"

"I was past feeling any pain. My whole body was numb and frantic all at the same time. The adrenaline was racing through my system. The tears wouldn't stop. They were talking but I couldn't understand anything that they were saying. I don't even know if they were talking to me."

"There was a sucking noise. I'll never forget that sound for as long as I live. I was thinking, 'this is sucking the life out of me.' And it was."

Now Angelina was sobbing harder. I was holding her close. Her body seemed so frail. She gasped in a couple of breaths and pressed on with an urgency to continue.

"I will always remember when the machine stopped sucking…and it was quiet," she whispered. "Since that time, I have never been comfortable with the quiet. I think that is why I fill my life with noise and chaos."

"The doctor told me that the procedure was over and he left the room. The nurse helped me to the dressing room and said that she would return when I was ready. She brought me papers to read. I left and vowed that I would never talk about that day again. You are the first person I have ever told what happened in that room. Even my husband never heard this story. I only relived this because I want you to know that it wasn't just a mass of cells. My baby was a perfectly-formed miniature baby, able to feel pain. That day I allowed them to take his or her life. I have lived with the knowledge of that ever since. Hear me Noelle. It was not a mass of cells!"

The tears fell from the eyes of a woman who was a total stranger to me; and yet, I felt like we had walked a path together. She cried. I'm not sure how long we were there and I don't know when it happened; but, I found myself standing beside her stool and rocking her gently.

I cradled her and said over and over, "I'm so sorry. I'm sorry that I've caused you to bring all of this to mind again. If I hadn't come here, you would not have had to do this."

Grabbing my shoulders Angelina gave me a little shake. "You listen to me," she said. "If telling this story will stop someone from doing what I did and having to live with these consequences all of their life, then what I did was not in vain. I can't bring my baby back; but, if one less baby has to die, then my baby's life had a purpose even after death.

"Angelina, I'm so scared and ashamed. I don't want my mom and sisters to know what I did. I don't want to disappoint them." I said.

"Honey, I know how you're feeling. I also know that even though you won't understand this now, those are minor emotions to deal with compared to living your whole life knowing that you took the life of the child that you were created to protect. Your mom instincts are to guard that child from danger, when that doesn't happen because of your own decisions, you're haunted. I know. When I see a child that's the same age…I always wonder, was the baby a girl or boy; blond hair and blue eyes or brown hair and green eyes? What will that baby think when we meet in Heaven? Has the baby forgiven me?"

"When you say that you're ashamed now; I can tell you that it's nothing compared to the shame that you'll feel after. That's a shame that never went away until I discovered that Jesus forgave me. Only that gave me the courage to lay that shame and remorse down. It's a shame that no one but Jesus can heal you from. I know. The weight of that burden is almost more than a person can bear." Angelina took a deep cleansing breath.

"I have some material that I picked up a while ago from a local pregnancy center when I was dropping off supplies to them. I wasn't sure why I was taking it; but now I know that God knew why. I want you to read it. I'm going to go and take a bath and spend some time with my Savior. I'm feeling the need to talk with Him. When I come back, we'll continue this conversation. Okay?" She smiled at me.

"Okay." I said and I hugged her one more time.

She walked to the desk in the kitchen and pulled some pamphlets out of the drawer. As she handed them to me she said, "I wish I had been given these years ago…you know…before."

"I know. You go and soak and I promise that I'll read through these while you're gone."

Turning and starting up the stairs, Angelina suddenly looked back, "Don't think that God hasn't forgiven me for what I did. He has. Knowing that is the only way that I've survived. I know that once I repented and called on the name of Jesus, He stood as intercessor for me with the Heavenly Father. Because of the work that Jesus did on the cross, I'm covered by His blood and the Father sees me white as snow. Only by the shedding of His blood can I be forgiven."

She turned back and I watched until she was gone. My thoughts were so jumbled; I don't know if I can do what she did. But in the back of my mind I still wasn't sure that it wasn't the answer for me. I didn't know if I could do anything differently.

After washing my dishes in the sink, I went to the couch and cuddled down into the pillows and opened the first booklet and began to read.

CHAPTER 12

PSALM 24:1-6
The earth is the LORD'S and everything in it,
the world, and all who live in it,
for He founded it upon the seas
and established it upon the waters.
Who may ascend the hill of the LORD?
Who may stand in His holy place?
He who has clean hands and a pure heart,
who does not lift up His soul to an idol
or swear by what is false.
He will receive blessing from the LORD
and vindication from His Savior
Such is the generation of those who seek Him
Who seek Your face, O God of Jacob.

DOING HIS WILL

ANGELINA FILLED THE TUB AS FULL AS SHE COULD WITH WAter as hot as she could stand. She sunk into the bubbles and let the tears flow. Cleansing tears; tears that mingled with the soapy water in the tub. Her heart was heavy from the trip into the past. Years ago she had given those thoughts to the Lord. They had been too hard for her to continue to carry around. In the beginning, she would take that sin to the cross and lay it at the feet of Jesus and then satan would rear his ugly head and remind her of what she had done. All over again she would remember and then she would be that broken woman who lived with the self condemnation of the sins of her past.

Then one day she had gone to a healing conference at a near by church and they taught her how to press into Jesus closer. She learned, not just in her head but also in her heart, how Jesus saw her white as snow after she repented. Those sins of the past are as far as the "east is from the west".

Romans 5:6 You see, at just the right time, when we were still powerless, Christ died for the ungodly. That spoke to her. She was ungodly and she needed a Savior. It went on to say in Romans 5:8 But God demonstrates His own love for us in this: While we were still sinners, Christ died for us. God sent His son to die on that cross even when I was still a sinner. He who knew my sins even before I knew them and still loved us enough to sacrifice His Son. The beauty of this continues in Romans 5:9 Since we have now been justified (which means—just as if we had never sinned) by His blood, how much more shall we be saved from God's wrath through Him! For if, when we were God's enemies, we were reconciled to Him through the death of His Son, how much more, having been reconciled, shall we be saved through His life! Not only is this so, but we also rejoice in God through our Lord Jesus Christ, through whom we have now received reconciliation.

Angelina thought about how that conference had been a turning point in her life. Even though she knew the truth, she had allowed satan to come and steal her peace often. From that day on she stood on the Word of God and when satan tried to destroy her, she would remind him of who was Lord of her life and what He had done for her.

Not that she ever forgot the life of that child or didn't wonder about what purpose God had created that baby for. She did. But, she learned how to live in the arms of Christ instead of in the grip of satan.

However, today had been hard. To have to relive that day so vividly, as she had never done before was almost more than she could humanly do. She knew that Christ was with her and that everything has a purpose. If telling her story can help Noelle make a decision for life, then the pain of today will all be worth it.

Angelina prayed: Heavenly Father, thank you for giving me the strength to do what I just did. It is only with your love, grace, and mercy that I got through it. Now I ask that You bury those words into Noelle's heart and use them to help her to make a decision of life for the precious baby that she's carrying. Father, please calm her nerves and help her to see the possibilities of choosing life. I pray that You are opening her mind so that she can hear Your words. Use us anyway that You see fit. We are Your humble servants and we praise Your Holy Name! Hallelujah to the King! Amen.

Angelina closed her eyes and continued to pray. As she did, she felt the reassurance of the Holy Spirit filling her. She knew that she had done the right thing and was basking in the time that she spent with her Savior. She was allowing her loving Father to heal the wound that had been broken open after so many years. Plus, she was giving Noelle time to think about all that she had said. Angelina prayed that Noelle was hearing the voice of the Lord so that He could lead her in the right direction.

* * * *

Sitting in class, Brad was going through the motions of being a good student. However, his mind was back at the farm. He was wondering how things were going with his mom and Noelle. He had gotten up earlier than usual this morning so that he could spend extra time praying for the both of them. He knew after last night that this was going to be a hard morning for his mom.

These were the times when he longed for the wisdom of his dad. Brad couldn't help wondering what today would have been like for his mom if his Dad could only be here to comfort her. I *know how much she misses you Dad. We all miss you.* He jolted back into reality wondering if he had said that out loud. No one was looking at him as if he were crazy, so he must be safe.

As he was reading this morning in his Bible, he went to one of his favorite verses, **Philippians 3:14 Forgetting what is behind and straining toward what is ahead, I press on toward the goal to win the prize for which God has called me heavenward in Christ Jesus.** So many stop there; but, Brad like to continue. **Philippians 3:15-16 All of us who are mature should take such a view of things. And if on some point you think differently, that too God will make clear to you. Only let us live up to what we have already attained.** What we forget is that life is a progress and it is through that journey that we become who God created us to be. It is the good and the bad that molds us. Brad's mind continued to focus on what he had read this morning. Forgetting what is behind. Mom had done that hadn't she? And now whatever that entailed, it was all coming to the surface again. He felt the need to pray for his mom again. *Father, be with her. Allow her the strength to do Your will and then help her to find Your peace again.*

The bell must have rang and Brad hadn't even heard it. Class was over and everyone was getting up and leaving. Brad didn't have a clue what had just happened.

"Hey Matt," Brad yelled.

"What's up?" Matt, another guy in the class, turned to face Brad.

"Man, I got lost back there. Do we have an assignment for the next class?"

"Sure do. Read the next chapter and write a paper on something in your life that relates." Matt said.

"Thanks. I don't seem to be myself today."

"No problem. Want to go down the road to grab some

lunch?"

"Thanks man; but I think I had better spend some time with the books. I'll take a rain check though."

"Absolutely." Matt waved as he headed down the hallway.

Brad headed to the cafeteria. He had a couple of hours to kill before his next class. This would give him time to read the assignment and decide what he was going to write. He was really enjoying this creative writing class.

As he ate the cookies that he had bought with a cup of coffee, his mind went back to yesterday and the look of Noelle curled up resting so peacefully on the couch. He wondered about the emotion that welled up in him as he looked at her. He had never met a girl that had ever made him feel that way. There was a protective spirit that he could not explain. He had been in situations before where girls had needed his help. This was different though. Before he was just going through the motions and getting the job done. He couldn't put his finger on why this was different. From somewhere deep inside he wanted to protect her. He wanted to make everything better and stop whatever was hurting her. These were new feelings for him. And instead of reading, he couldn't help but continue to mull them over.

After this next class, he would head back to the farm and pick up Noelle and they would go into town and get the tire. He would take her over to the restaurant and buy her lunch and then what? Back to the farm and she would be gone. Would he ever see her again? Somehow that wasn't okay. But what was okay? He knew nothing about her. He didn't know where she came from or where she was going. What he did know was that she was a broken little girl disguised as a woman. And she was in trouble. That much was clear. There was so much confusion in his thoughts that he did the only thing that he knew would help.

Father, today seems to be a day that I need you more than

ever. I don't know what these feelings are all about; but You do. I'm just asking that You guide me in all ways. I know that You always have a plan and I don't want to get in the way of You. Be with all of us on this day and show us the direction that You're going with all of this. If I never see Noelle after today, protect her and help her to grow closer to You. Bless her life in ways that only You can. Thank you Father for being there even when we don't understand. Amen.

Brad checked his watch, gathered his books, and headed to his last class of the day. Hopefully he would be more attentive during this session than he had been during the last. He was eager to get this class behind him and be on his way home.

CHAPTER 13

PSALM 91:14-16
"Because he loves me," says the LORD,
"I will rescue him;
I will protect him, for he acknowledges my name.
He will call upon me, and I will answer him;
I will be with him in trouble,
I will deliver him and honor him.
With long life will I satisfy him
and show him my salvation."

LISTENING FOR HIS VOICE

NOELLE LOOKED AT THE BOOKLETS. SHE NOTICED THAT they were from "Focus on the Family". She thought that sounded familiar. Then she remembered that she had listened to their radio program before. One caught her eye. "What Does God Say About Abortion?" She opened it up and began to read.

The first page asked a question "Why should we value life?" Then it listed these scriptures:

> ***In the beginning God created the heavens and the earth. Genesis 1:1***
>
> ***So God created man in His own image, in the image of God He created Him; male and female He created them. Genesis 1:27***
>
> ***From one man He made every nation of men that they should inhabit the whole earth;***

> ***and He determined the times set for them and the exact places where they should live. Acts 17:26***

So in other words what the Bible is saying is that God determined life; including the life that is growing inside of me. In fact this life is created in the mirror image of God? Noelle pondered that.

It went on with:

> ***Knowing that the LORD is God. It is He who made us, and we are His; we are His people, the sheep of His pasture. Psalm 100:3***
>
> ***This is what the LORD says—your Redeemer, who formed you in the womb: I am the LORD, who has made all things, who alone stretched out the heavens, who spread out the earth by myself. Isaiah 44:24***
>
> ***For by Him all things were created: things in heaven and on earth, visible and invisible, whether thrones or powers or rulers or authorities all things were created by Him and for Him. Colossians 1:16***
>
> ***Yet, O LORD, You are our Father. We are the clay, You are the potter; we are all the work of Your hand. Isaiah 64:8***

I get all of that. I've been to church and I know that God is God; but, what am I supposed to do? I have to think about my mom and sisters. Then she heard a small voice inside ask, "Is this about them, or is this about you?"

Noelle paused. *Okay…I'm scared. I'll admit it.*

Then there was question number two, "Who is the Creator of the unborn?"

> ***Did not He who made me in the womb make them? Did not the same one form us both within our mother? Job 31:15***
>
> ***Your hands shaped me and made me. Will You now turn and destroy me? Remember that You molded me like clay. Will You now turn me to dust again? Did You not pour me out like milk and curdle me like cheese, clothe me with skin and flesh and knit me together with bones and sinews? You gave me life and showed me kindness, and in Your providence watched over my spirit. Job 10:8-12***
>
> ***For You created my inmost being; You knit me together in my mother's womb. I praise You because I am fearfully and wonderfully made; Your works are wonderful, I know that full well. My frame was not hidden from You when I was made in the secret place. When I was woven together in the depths of the earth, Your eyes saw my unformed body. All the days ordained for me were written in Your book before one of them came to be. Psalm 139:13-16***

Are you saying that this baby has already been recorded in Your book Lord? Noelle began to talk to the Lord as if He was right beside her. This was new for her. She had never really considered that a big God was able to be personal with her.

She continued through the book with question three, "How is God concerned with the unborn?"

> ***Listen to me, you islands; hear this, you distant nations: Before I was born the LORD called me; from my birth He has made mention of my name. Isaiah 49:1***
>
> ***Before I formed You in the womb I knew***

> ***you, before you were born I set you apart; I appointed you as a prophet to the nations. Jeremiah 1:5***

Lord am I understanding Your word to say that You know us before conception; that You even have appointed a plan for our lives? This baby already has a purpose? Noelle was becoming uncomfortable. This isn't what she wanted to hear. She had a plan! What about her plan?

> ***Praise be to the God and Father of our Lord Jesus Christ, who has blessed us in the heavenly realms with every spiritual blessing in Christ. For He chose us in Him before the creation of the world to be holy and blameless in His sight. Ephesians 1:3-4***

Holy and blameless in His sight. That takes me out of the picture. I have already created the sin. This baby is the consequences to that sin. Noelle struggled with self condemnation. *I have already failed You Lord.*

Be still and know that I am God.

Again the voice spoke to her; He spoke all the way to the depths of her. She was becoming confused. She knew people who believed that God was personal to them. She had just never seen the need. Or maybe she had ignored His calling to her.

Question four, "Who is responsible for life and death?"

> ***The LORD brings death and makes alive; He brings down to the grave and raises up. 1 Samuel 2:6***

> ***And God spoke all these words…"You shall not murder". Exodus 20:1, 13***

> ***"You have heard that it was said to the***

> ***people long ago, 'Do not murder, and anyone who murders will be subject to judgment.'" Matthew 5:21***

> ***Jesus replied, "'Do not murder, do not commit adultery, do not steal, do not give false testimony, honor your father and mother' and 'love your neighbor as yourself.'" Matthew 19:19***

> ***If you do not oppress the alien, the fatherless or the widow and do not shed innocent blood in this place, and if you do not follow other gods to your own harm, then I will let you live in this place, in the land I gave your forefathers for ever and ever. Jeremiah 7:6-7***

Lord does that apply to me? Are you saying that if I have an abortion, that I would be responsible for shedding innocent blood?

> ***This is what the LORD says: Do what is just and right. Rescue from the hand of his oppressor the one who has robbed. Do no wrong or violence to the alien, the fatherless or the widow, and do not shed innocent blood in this place. Jeremiah 22:3***

Every verse began to feel to Noelle like it had been written for this moment and for this time.

> ***This day I call heaven and earth as witness against you that I have set before you life and death, blessings and curses. Now choose life, so that you and your children may live...Deuteronomy 30:19***

Wow Lord! You're saying that You are giving me the right to make this choice; but, that I'll have to live with the blessings or curses that come with the choice I make. Lord...this is too hard.

Noelle began to scan further into the booklet when a scripture jumped out at her.

> ***Fathers shall not be put to death for their children, nor children put to death for their fathers; each is to die for his own sin. Deuteronomy 24:16***

Noelle read that again and again. It became very clear at that point. This baby could not be held accountable for the poor choices that Noelle had made. She could not consider an abortion. But then what? What was she supposed to do now?

Lord, I don't know what to do? I don't even know how to ask for Your help? I don't want to do something that would cause me the pain that I have seen in Angelina today. But... how Lord, how? I don't know how to take care of a baby. I'd be on my own. This baby would be a reminder of everything that I did wrong. It would be a reminder of the ugliness that was done to me that night. I don't want to live the rest of my life remembering that. What would I see when I looked into the face of that little one? And then there is my family. How do I tell my family about what happened? What about the responsibility that I have to my sisters? There is so much that I don't understand. Help me...please.

Noelle prayed as she had never prayed before. She continued to beg God for understanding. From the recesses of her mind, a scripture verse that she had learned years ago at a summer Vacation Bible School began to resound in her.

> ***Trust in the Lord with all your heart and lean not on your own understanding; in all your ways acknowledge Him, and He will make your paths straight. Proverbs 3:5-6***

Lord, I know that verse. I learned that when I was a little girl. Noelle began to repeat the verse over and over. As she did, strength began to grow in her.

Father, are you telling me that You want me to trust You? How do I do that? This is so new to me. But I can see how Your hand has directed me these last few days. Only You could have loved me, and this baby, enough to have guided my destination to this home of Your people. Angelina and Brad have shown me who You are in a way that is so real. You were there even in the little things like the CD that played in the car that I bought. Your words played over and over as I drove. Those words were washing over me; filling me with Your grace and mercy.

Father, forgive me for the sin that I committed. Forgive me for having put myself in a place where this could happen. Have mercy on me for the sexual sin that caused this problem. Father I stepped out of your will for my life and I know that this is the consequence to that sin. Lord give me the strength not to commit a bigger sin by looking for a way out of this problem that will take me farther away from You. Help me not to be selfish. Help me to be selfless. Father, I need You. And Father forgive me for hating the boy that did this to me.

****

Angelina found Noelle sitting on the couch with her head bent and her eyes closed. She thought that she was asleep until she saw her lips moving and saw the tears that were falling down her cheeks. As deep calls to deep, Angelina's spirit called to Noelle's. She quietly moved and knelt in front of her. Taking Noelle's hands into hers she began to pray with her. Time slipped away as they both rested in His healing arms. Angelina knew that Noelle was hearing His voice and that her life was changing.

"We thank you Lord for Your faithfulness. Father please don't leave her. She is going to need more of You." Angelina prayed.

Looking up Noelle spoke quietly, "Angelina, I can't consider an abortion. I understand now that God already has a plan for this baby. But, I'm so scared. How do I know what to do?" Noelle looked like a little girl herself.

"Honey, whenever I have a trial to walk through I try to look only at one moment at a time. I can't look down the road or it's too overwhelming." She answered as she came up on the couch and wrapped her arms around Noelle.

"I don't know how to do this. Tell me what to do." She cried softly.

"Okay, let's look at where we are and see if we can decide the next step that has to be taken." Noelle nodded at her. "My thought is about your mom coming home and finding you gone. You don't really want that to happen do you? She's going to be so worried."

"What can I do about it? I'm here and I left a letter for her to read that said I needed to leave for awhile and that I would call her when I had everything figured out."

"Well…what time would you expect that she would be home?" Angelina asked.

Noelle thought for a moment and said, "Depending on what time they left my aunt's house, it's a four hour drive to our house. So they could get home anytime after noon I would guess. I'm pretty sure that since Mom hasn't been able to reach me; she'll want to leave fairly early."

"Do you have an answering machine?"

"Yes."

"Then, I think, that the best you can do is call and leave her a message. Ask her to call here as soon as she returns. I would suggest that you ask her not to read the letter until after she's talked with you." Angelina could see the struggle going on in Noelle. "Honey one thing at a time. Don't borrow trouble. Don't second guess what your mom is going to say. Don't even think about it. Just ask the Lord to lead and then you follow. Okay?"

"Okay", was the shaky reply from Noelle's lips.

Angelina continued with, "Then when Brad gets home, we'll send him into town to take care of your tire and he can pop over to the restaurant and help out there. We'll wait for your mom's call here."

"But you need…"

"Shhhhh. I need to do exactly what the Lord wants me to do. And for now He has been gracious enough to allow me the opportunity to help you."

"What will I say to Mom?"

"Don't get in front of the Lord. Remember…let Him lead. He won't lead you astray. Let's pray and ask Him to prepare you and your mother for the conversations to come."

"Father, we are Your humble servants and we are seeking after You for direction. Please Father give Noelle the words to talk with her mother about everything that has happened in the last four days. Be with her mom and give her supernatural ears to hear the way that You hear. Let the message be delivered with love and received with love. Bind this family together through You in a way that they have never known You before. We trust You. Father, Your word tells us that if we trust in You with all of our heart, that You will direct our path. Father, we wait for that direction. In Jesus name. Amen."

Angelina opened her eyes and Noelle said excitedly, "When I was praying before you came down, I remembered that verse, Proverbs 3:5-6. My sisters and I would go with our friends to our local church for a VBS summer program years ago. It was as if I could hear it inside of me.

"God's like that. ***I Peter 1:25 The word of the Lord stands forever.*** Then in ***John 1:1 In the beginning was the Word, and the Word was with God, and Word was God.*** So when we bury His word in our hearts it's there forever. Then when we ask, the Holy Spirit, or God living in us, calls it to our remembrance. That should tell you that even after all of those years, He's been just waiting for you to call on Him. Have you ever asked the Lord into your heart?"

"Yes, that was years ago also. And it was at another VBS program. All of my friends, we all went forward together. I think that I was in sixth grade. But, my family only went to church on the holidays or special occasions. I guess there was always something else to do."

Noelle looked lost in time for a few minutes, "It could have been so different for me, and my family, if we'd only made God a priority in our lives; very different." Noelle shrugged her shoulders. "That's a story for another day."

"It doesn't matter. Our God never leaves us or forsakes us. He's just rejoicing that you came today." Angelina continued with, "Honey, why don't you go upstairs and take a nap. I'm going to make some pies to send to the restaurant with Brad. If the phone rings, I'll bring it to you."

"How can I thank you?" Again Noelle asked.

"Not necessary. If only someone had told me the truth; it could have saved my baby. Now you go and rest."

CHAPTER 14

PSALM 6:9
The LORD has heard my cry for mercy;
The LORD accepts my prayer.

HOLDING ONTO A LIFELINE

NOELLE SLOWLY SANK INTO THE SOFT BED AND WRAPPED the covers tightly around her; she closed her eyes and almost felt like arms were holding her tight. She wanted to go back to the days of her youth where her daddy would come home and take her onto his lap and smother her with kisses saying, "You are my first princess and you will always be my first princess". She wanted to go back to the days before her daddy would never come home again. In those days she didn't have to think about telling her mom how she had made choices that were going to change her life.

She laid her hand on her tummy and for the first time considered that there was actually a life growing inside of her that God had created. Before today it wasn't really a life; it was just a problem that she had to deal with; a problem that was causing her grief. But…not now. Now she knew better. She knew that life had begun to grow and develop into what God had planned. A life that was physically dependent on her. She began to wonder about this life inside of her. Was the baby a boy or girl? Did the baby understand that she was her mother? Did she feel safe? Does a baby have thoughts? Would this baby have known that her mother was planning on eliminating her life?

Noelle shuddered at the thought. The tears slowly slipped from her eyes onto the pillow as she stroked her tummy and said, "Baby, I'm so sorry for what I was thinking. I promise you today that I will do all that I can do to protect you. I know that what happened wasn't your fault. I don't know how all of this is going to turn out. But, I do know that you will be the most important consideration from this moment on. I'll make sure that you get a good start towards fulfilling the plans that 'God has for your life'".

That being said, Noelle felt like she had actually turned a corner. She knew that whatever she did, the baby had to come first. She had to find a way to explain to her mom that…One: she was pregnant and Two: she was going to have the baby, and Three: what was three going to be? Was this baby created to be hers? Was she only to carry this baby to delivery and give the baby to a family who God had waiting? She didn't know. This much she had learned today though; she would not get ahead of God. He had given her so much already through Angelina that she was becoming more confident in Him. She was at peace that He would also give her the next step and the next and the next…as she slowly drifted off to sleep.

* * * *

Angelina busied herself making pies for the restaurant's supper crowd. She had planned to make them when she went into work today. Now her plans had changed and she knew that God wanted her here as support for Noelle. She wasn't upset at all. In fact she felt light inside. She was sure that as she had spoken God's words to Noelle today new life had been saved.

God, I want to thank you for bringing Noelle to our family. I'm so grateful that You gave me the opportunity to be Your servant. Be with Noelle's mom and prepare her for what she's about to find out. Father, give Noelle the strength to say the words that she'll have to say. Let those words be accepted with love and caring. And may the life of that baby be brought to fruition; to be held by loving parents who will understand the gift that they have been given. Father give Noelle peace as she decides whether to keep the baby or give the baby to a couple who are desperately waiting with open arms. You know best Lord. We trust You for Your direction. In Jesus Name. Amen.

Just as Angelina finished praying, the pies that filled her double ovens were done. She was putting the finishing touches on the cream pies as Brad walked into the house.

"Boy, does it smell good in here. I hope that some of those are for us." He said.

"Oh…I may have worked my fingers to the bone to make one just for you", was her sassy reply.

He came over and kissed his mother's cheek. "How has your morning been?"

She smiled at the son who had always been so much like his father. She could always count on Brad to be considerate of everyone else's feelings. She was sure that he had been praying for her today.

"Today has been hard and wonderful all at the same time. Noelle and I have shared some very personal talks and I think that God has really grabbed a hold of that girl. I was just thanking Him for letting us be used in her life."

With that said, she shifted gears and jumped into giving instructions. "Because of what Noelle is going to have to do today, I think that it is more important that I stay here with her. However, to do that I'm going to need some help at the restaurant. I was hoping that you could take Noelle's tire into town and get that fixed and then head over to help with the evening crowd. I'm still short help today; although, I've made all of the pies here that they are going to need for the supper hour."

Brad could feel the disappointment creep in. He was really looking forward to spending the afternoon with this girl that was invading so many of his thoughts. But, he also knew that his mother would not ask if it wasn't what she thought was best.

"You bet. If that's what you need me to do, I'll head out right away. Where is Noelle?" He asked.

"It's been an exhausting morning for both of us and she's going to have more emotional times yet today; so I sent her up to rest for a while. Brad I would share with you what's going on; but, I really feel that it isn't my place to fill you in. I think that Noelle should have the right to tell who she chooses to tell." Angelina shrugged at her son.

"Nope, that's okay Mom. I understand. If she wants to tell me, then I'll be here when she's ready. I already have the tire loaded so let me go and change my shirt. I'll leave as soon as the pies are done."

"They're done. I'll have them packaged up by the time that you're ready to leave." She walked over and gave her son a quick hug.

"What's that for?" He asked with a smirk.

"Oh nothing…I just hope you know that your dad would be very proud of who you and Eyan have become. Thanks for being so much like him. He may be gone; but he left me a piece of him in you and your brother. I really needed that today." She smiled and as her eyes sparkled with tears, she turned to finish wrapping the pies.

Brad headed up the stairs that blurred in front of him.

CHAPTER 15

PSALM 27:1-5

The LORD is my light and my salvation—
whom shall I fear?
The LORD is the stronghold of my life—
of whom shall I be afraid?
When evil men advance against me to devour my flesh,
when my enemies and my foes attack me,
they will stumble and fall.
Though an army besiege me, my heart will not fear;
though war break out against me,
even then will I be confident.
One thing I ask of the LORD, this is what I seek;
That I may dwell in the house of the LORD
all the days of my life,
To gaze upon the beauty of the LORD
and to seek Him in His temple.
For in the day of trouble
He will keep me safe in His dwelling;
He will hide me in the shelter of His tabernacle
and set me high upon a rock.

THE CLOUD OF FEAR

"WHY DO I HAVE THIS UNEASY FEELING?" GENIE SMITH asked herself. Something had not been sitting in her spirit well for days. She was sure that the feeling had to do with her oldest daughter Noelle. She had not talked with her since saying good-bye at their home before leaving on this visit to see her sister. That in itself was not enough to cause this unease; but neither of the girls had heard from her either.

In thinking back, Noelle had been very quiet for quite awhile. It was true this new college life was taxing and would take some getting used to. So for that reason she hadn't pushed her for answers. Noelle had always been an over achiever. She likes to have all of her ducks in a row and she doesn't like surprises. This last year with the changes in their family unit had been hard on all of them. She could see where it was exceptionally hard on Noelle. How was she supposed to handle going from being a daddy's girl and then over night not even having a daddy. That would be a hard adjustment for any girl.

Genie had thought that they were doing a great job of figuring it all out. We had each other and we all talked about our feelings openly. Well maybe not at first. In the beginning we didn't know how to talk about it. First we had to process and accept that it had even happened. They couldn't understood why their dad had left. What could I tell them? I was as much in the dark as they were. I went to a counselor who helped me work through my emotions and then I went home and talked with the girls. We considered family counseling; and decided against it. The girls were busy and we had each other. We thought that was enough. So we talked to each other. And a year went by. We are still here and surviving. Genie's thoughts were that we must be doing something right.

Yet, four days go by and I can't get a hold of Noelle. Questions begin to go though my mind. Is she okay? Is she really handling the change as well as I think that she is? Should I have done something differently? I wonder over and over if I should have done more. Am I just fooling myself to think that they are adjusting as well as I am thinking that they are?

Today we'll be back home and maybe I can put some of this to rest. I'm going to have a more in depth conversation with that oldest daughter of mine. I'm going to make sure that she's moving forward in a healthy way and that she isn't shouldering unnecessary burdens. Surely, she isn't feeling responsible for her sisters or for me. We can take care of each other; but I will not have anyone of us feeling like we have to carry the responsibilities for their dad's actions. He made those choices on his own without our input. And he certainly didn't think twice about how those choices were going to affect our lives or he would have done things differently.

No…today Noelle and I will sit and have a good old fashioned heart to heart. I will listen carefully to what she is saying and to what she may not be saying. Then I'll make sure that she knows how much we love her and that we're all going to be okay.

That being decided, Genie relaxed a little and enjoyed the chatter of the girls in the car as they drove home. They all had enjoyed their time away. The only way that it could have been more perfect was if Noelle had been with them. Next time they would not leave home without her.

Nissa and Anaya were laughing at the craziness of the past few days. Nissa and her Aunt Debbie had decided that they would stop in every store in the outlet mall. So they took off on a dead run and actually was able to cover miles of stores in the two days. For them it was a race. Anaya and her mom had decided to make it a marathon of a leisurely pace. They selectively mapped out their path. They were each on their way home with some really great buys that they were excited about. Nissa, on the other hand, had purchased basically nothing. She had shopped all weekend and had almost nothing to show for it.

"Well at least we're the same size so that I can borrow some of the stuff that you bought," Nissa said with a begging smile.

"Okay," said Anaya, "but only after I wear it first. Between you and Noelle, I can never find my clothes." We all laughed at that. Anaya was the most unorganized of all of the girls and she could not find her stuff regardless of what anybody else did.

"Seriously? You can't really believe that Noelle and I are your problem. No one keeps a messier room than you do. Maybe that's why we can't get a hold of Noelle. She probably went into your room and can't find her way out."

The mention of Noelle brought Genie's thoughts back to her daughter.

"Girls, have either of you noticed anything different about Noelle lately?" I asked.

"Well now that you mention it Mom," Anaya said, "I think that she has been sort of quiet. Like she was only going through the motions of being with us; but was really somewhere else. Like maybe there was something on her mind that she's not talking about."

Genie pondered what Anaya said. If anyone would notice it would be Anaya. Noelle and her sister had always had a special bond. Not that Nissa was left out. It was just that being the oldest and the youngest they seemed to be more connected. I think that there is really some truth in that 'middle child syndrome'. Nissa always seemed to be marching to a different beat than the other girls.

"I think that it's just hard starting college. That's enough to make anyone anxious. I know that I'll feel over whelmed when I start college. There's safety in going to school where you have always been and where everyone knows and accepts you. College is stepping out of your comfort zone. She'll be okay once she gets through this first semester. By then she'll have figured it out and relaxed a little." Nissa said.

I smiled at Nissa across the seat from me. "I'm sure that

you're right. So let's all make an effort to help her any way that we can for a while giving her the time to focus on her studies." The girls nodded their agreement and then quieted down and within minutes they were sound asleep, resting after the rush of the last four days.

* * * *

Four hours later, and weary from travel, we were finally pulling into the driveway of our home. As I pushed the remote to the garage door opener, the girls began to stretch and move from their naps.

"Wow! That trip went fast." Nissa said through her yawn.

"I know. It doesn't even feel like I just drove four hours all by myself." I wink at her sleepy, sweet face.

The girls chime in together a half hearted, "sorry Mom".

"You go ahead. Anaya and I will carry in the packages and suitcases." Nissa said, though I barely acknowledged her as I headed for the house door.

As I open the door, I'm calling out to Noelle. "Noelle", I call out for a second time. I walk up the stairs and still I'm not finding her. She could be out with friends or at the school studying. The possibilities are numerous. Still that nagging feeling rushes through my spirit. I want to see my daughter and know that she's okay. I want to laugh with her and join in as the girls relay the fun of the time away. I don't want to wait one more minute to be reassured that everything is alright.

I begin to notice that the house is in the same order that I left it in and that doesn't set well with me. Everything looks the same. Not one thing is out of place. The house looks like no one has lived in it. Noelle is neat, but not that neat. I'm beginning to feel a knot in the pit of my stomach. I go to the kitchen where there's a white board that we use to leave each other messages. There is nothing on the board. The knot is getting bigger and I'm starting to feel clammy and sick.

Thoughts begin to run through my mind that no mother should ever think. “Stop it!” I say to myself. I go to the phone and the red light is blinking at me. I push it and quickly scroll through the multitude of voices that are not Noelle’s and then I hear her.

“Mom”, there is a long pause, “if you’re hearing this after reading the letter that I left, I’m sorry. If you haven’t read the letter yet…please don’t. Not until you talk to me. I need you to call me at this number first. Please…please do not read the letter before you call me. I want to explain. If you have read the letter, call me anyway. We need to talk. I love you and I’ll be waiting for your call.”

The message was over and I realized that I had been holding my breath. I took a couple of deep breaths and played the message again. This time I recorded the number that was on the machine taking note that the number is a different area code and not a number that I recognize. The girls are busting through the door just in time to catch the last of the message and they want to hear all of it so we play it again.

We all look at each other with a quizzical look wondering what all of that was about. The one thing that I knew was that I was going to call the number; but first I was going to find that letter. I went straight to my bedroom where I assumed she would have known that I would find the letter and there it was on my bed. I pick it up and start to open it.

“Wait!” Nissa and Anaya yell right behind me. “You can’t open that.” Nissa says.

“Oh…yes I can. I want to know what’s in this letter.” I said.

“No Mom!” Anaya says. “Whatever Noelle wrote in that letter she now wants to tell you in person. You can’t open that knowing that she specifically asked you not to.”

I knew what the girls were saying was true. But I wanted to know right now what was up with my daughter.

"Whatever it is can wait a few minutes. Waiting isn't going to change anything." Nissa says. I need a few minutes and so do you. We want to be there when you call her. So let's get around and we'll call from the kitchen phone in five minutes.

I hesitated long enough that they could see my indecision.

"Come on Mom. Give us the letter and we'll see you in the kitchen. It will be better that way. You wouldn't want Noelle to know that you opened the letter after she asked you not to…right?" Nissa asked me.

I knew that she was right so I handed over the letter and on my way into my bathroom I ordered, "five minutes…that's it".

CHAPTER 16

PSALM 38:17-18
For I am about to fall,
and my pain is ever with me.
I confess my iniquity;
I am troubled by my sin.

FACING THE HARD STUFF

NOELLE WOKE FROM HER NAP KNOWING THE FIRST STEP WAS talking with her mom. She could almost feel the nudging of the Lord. Angelina was right. God really would help her walk through this if she asked Him to.

Working her way out from under the warm covers, she went into the bathroom and washed her face and brushed her teeth. An intoxicating aroma greeted her at the top of the stairs and she followed it down the steps and into the kitchen.

Angelina heard her coming before she saw her. She turned with a smile and said, "Come over here and sit. I have your lunch ready. How does homemade soup with oven fresh rolls and fresh fruit and dip for desert sound?"

"Like I may have died and gone to heaven." Noelle joked. "If I am here much longer, I won't be able to button my pants around me…food or not."

"Silly girl! Now what do you want to drink with your soup? I have milk, tea, juice and I would offer you pop; but I don't think that would be the best choice for a girl growing a healthy baby." Angelina grinned.

Feeling a little embarrassed, Noelle said milk would be great and thanked Angelina for the wonderful meal.

"So, I've been thinking about all that you've said and all that I read this morning and I'm ready to talk with my mom. I'm just not sure how to do this. Do I tell her everything over the phone? Would you want to get this kind of news from a phone call? What do you think?"

Angelina felt the pride for this girl welling up inside of her. She was really getting it. Answering her she said, "I don't think that I would want to learn this over the phone. As a mom, I would want to see your face and be able to hug you and hold you close. So we do seem to have a dilemma, don't we? Let me think a minute on this." She paused while weighing the problem.

"How far away do you live?" She asked.

"I don't really know. I just got in the car and started driving. I wasn't driving very fast. I took back roads whenever possible. I don't even know which direction I went except that I stated out going north."

"Let's look at a map and see where you live from here." Angelina went to the closet and pulled out an atlas. "We're here at Hadley, Indiana. This is a suburb of Indianapolis. So where is your home?"

Looking bewildered Noelle answered, "We live in Atlanta, Georgia".

"Atlanta, Georgia! Girl? Do you know how far you drove?" Angelina began thanking God for bringing Noelle this far.

She continued, "This is just a thought. Would your mom be able to fly here? She could stay with us and you could talk with her face to face. I have a tendency to be helpful to a fault. You just say stop anytime that you feel like I'm running over the top of you." Angelina shrugged her shoulders as if to apologize.

"Stop it. I can't thank you enough for what you have done for me and this baby."

Angelina took note that she still didn't refer to the baby as hers.

"When I left home, I was headed anywhere that I could get an abortion and start to put this all behind me. I just wanted to cover it all up before my family found out. God dropped me right into your arms and I will always be grateful. I just don't know what to do next. I do know that whatever happens, I will give this baby a chance to live up to the potential that God has for him…or her. I didn't understand. As I look back, I think that God was helping me find the truth. Think about it…I could have ended up anywhere with anyone. But, I'm here with a family that knew Him and was willing to share."

She continued, "I would love it if my mom would fly here. But, it isn't fair to you. I've already inconvenienced you so much. I would feel better if…

"Now you stop it." Angelina scolded. "It would not be an inconvenience." I like to think that I have the gift of hospitality. This is my service to the Lord so don't you dare try to steal my blessing.

Noelle was just about to comment when the phone rang and they both knew who was calling.

* * * *

Genie's hands were so wet from perspiration that she could barely hold the phone. Her stomach felt like there was a rock sitting in the bottom of it. She was trying to make a definite decision to breathe normally. She knew in her spirit that something was terribly wrong with her oldest. In her head she was counting the rings. One…Two…Three.

"Hello." Angelina answered.

"Yes, my name is Genie Smith and my daughter left this number on my answering machine for me to call."

"Hi Genie; my name is Angelina Conroy and I've been having the most wonderful time with your daughter. Here let me put her on the phone so that you can talk with her." Angelina was stalling giving Noelle time to prepare for the ensuing conversation.

She walked over to the stools at the bar and handed Noelle the phone. She motioned that she was leaving and Noelle grabbed her arm and shot her a pleading look. She wanted her to stay. Angelina nodded okay.

"Mom; it's me. I'm sorry if I've worried you. I don't even know where to start. I guess I need to tell you that I love you very much and that I'm okay. Some wonderful things have happened to me; and some not so wonderful things. Mom; I thought that I needed to leave, to leave home; so I did. I was…I was running away to protect you and the girls. It wasn't such a good idea; but, I want to tell you about the wonderful way that God took care of me. I don't want to talk over the phone though. I know this is an inconvenience and I'm so sorry; but, could you come here?" Noelle felt like she was stumbling over her words.

"Honey, are you sure that you're okay. Are you telling me the truth? No one is making you say these things are they?"

"Oh no Mom, the people who are helping me have been wonderful. More wonderful than I can even express." Noelle looked at Angelina and smiled.

"Where are you?" Genie asked.

"I'm in a suburb of Indianapolis, Indiana." She answered.

"What? How did you get there?" Her mom did not hide she shock.

"It's a long story. Mom, can you come? The lady that you spoke with has kindly offered me a room. I spent last night here after having car trouble. She's offered you a room also. I know this must make no sense to you; but, I really need you to come."

"Car trouble? What car?"

"I'll explain everything when you get here. I just need you to come. I'm sorry Mom…I'm so sorry."

"Honey, if you need me, I'll be there as quick as I can. Are you okay while I make arrangements for the girls and get a ticket?

"Yes. I'm very safe and comfortable. I'm just so sorry."

"Stop it. Whatever the problem is, we can get through this together. Do you hear me? Nothing is going to change how much I love you. I won't allow anything to ever come between me and my girls. We are a team. Remember that. We're a team and we're going to stay that way. Okay? Promise me."

Noelle could hear the desperate plea in her mom's voice.

"I promise. I'll be right here waiting for you. Mom…can you come as quick as possible."

"I will be on the first flight out of here that I can get. I promise.

"Mom, do we have enough money for this?"

"We have whatever we need to make this okay; don't you worry about the money. I'll be okay as long as you're okay."

"Thanks Mom."

"Honey, I'll call you in a few minutes and let you know what time I'll be there."

"Okay, I'll wait for your call."

Angelina was mouthing that she should fly into the Indianapolis International Airport.

"Mom, you will need to fly into the Indianapolis airport. It's called the Indianapolis International Airport. We'll pick you up there." Noelle said.

Genie ventured a question, "Noelle what about the letter? Can I read it now?"

"No…please don't read the letter yet? You can bring it with you and we'll read it together. Okay. Please Mom…I'm so ashamed. Please don't read the letter?"

"It's okay Honey. I'll bring the letter with me. I promise I will wait for you before I open the letter. I love you, Noelle."

"I love you too, Mom. And Mom…thanks."

And with that Noelle hung up the phone and started to cry.

Genie could hear the tears starting in her daughter's voice. Her heart felt like it was breaking. She would get to her daughter as fast as she could.

Angelina came around the bar and wrapped her arms around the broken little girl sitting on her stool. She wanted so much to help. She knew that Noelle would think that she was doing one of the hardest things that she would ever do. She also knew that there could be harder times to come. For now she rocked back and forth with her as she cried. "It's going to be okay Honey. You are a brave girl and you did the right thing. We're just going to do one step at a time."

"My mom loves me and I've let her down. She is going to think this is her fault. It isn't. What is she going to think about me?"

"Noelle I don't know your mom; but, I can tell from how she handled the phone call, she's going to think that her daughter needs her and she'll love you even more."

"I hope so." Was all that Noelle could say.

CHAPTER 17

PSALM 5:1-3
Give ear to my words, O LORD,
consider my sighing.
Listen to my cry for help,
my King and my God,
for to You I pray.
In the morning, O LORD, You hear my voice;
In the morning I lay my requests before you
and wait in expectation.

THE LONG WAIT

BRAD HAD TO WONDER WHY HE WAS SO DISAPPOINTED THAT the afternoon plans had changed. He didn't question when his mom asked him to go into town by himself to take care of the tire. He knew that she wouldn't have asked him to work at the restaurant if she hadn't really needed to be at home. Whatever was going on in their home was important enough that Mom was willing to change all of her plans to make it happen. So he continued to pray for God's intervention in whatever it was.

When he got to the gas station, he just explained to Adam that he was needed at the restaurant today and that he would just leave the wheel.

"No problem. I'm meeting a friend for dinner there after I close. I'll just bring the tire with me and throw it in the back of your truck."

"That would great." Brad answered. Make sure you bring

the bill and I'll square up there.

With that taken care of, Brad headed over to unload the evening's desserts and find out where he could be used the most. He wasn't a stranger to the restaurant. He really enjoyed it. It gave him time to catch up with people that he didn't see as much anymore. He hoped today would be no exception. He thought that maybe he would need a lot of interaction to make the day go fast and keep his mind on the task at hand and not on what was going on back at the house.

Unloading the car and carefully carrying the goodies in, Brad was greeted by both workers and dinner guests. It looked like a full house even after the lunch crowd. The smell of the fresh baked pies filled the dining room and the crowd began to cheer. People yelled, "Angelina's done it again" and "no one does it like your mom". It was a family like atmosphere.

"Brad, your mom just called and told us that you were coming in to help. You don't know what a life saver you are. Here, let me help with that load." Barb, one of the cooks, was all smiles as he entered into the kitchen.

"None of this was unusual to Brad. He and his brother, Eyan, had been helping out at the restaurant since they were old enough to wash dishes. They both knew the routines as well as anyone there. So stepping into the flow of the crowd wasn't a challenge for him. This was a part of his heritage and he savored the time spent in the mix of the excitement.

Today was no exception. They put him to work waiting tables. Which, of all of the jobs, was Brad's favorite. They were settling into the evening crowd before he knew it. Brad was taking orders, getting drinks, delivering food, and then clearing tables after the diners were happily on their way. Sometimes it was just a quick stop for a cup of coffee and Angelina's famous pie. For others it was a family night out with the works.

Fortunately, Brad didn't have time to think about what was

happening back at the farm. There was always something to do. He refreshed the salad bar, refilled the dessert table, made sure that the floors got a good once over and that the tables were ready to go. His mom was a stickler for a tidy place for people to come, relax and enjoy a wonderful meal. She saw this not as a job or business; but this was a ministry. She was a servant and that was the attitude that she expected from all of the staff that worked here. Not that it was a burden for any of them. Angelina had a way of making everyone that was around her feel like family. More than once Brad had seen her in deep conversation with a customer or employee and then you would see them bow their heads and together pray for whatever need was happening at the time. No one was ever surprised. And everyone knew that if they asked for prayer it would be between them and Angelina. She was more than an entrepreneur; she was a prayer warrior. Sometimes Brad thought that the people came more for the prayer than they did for the food. The fact that the food was so good was just an added bonus.

Brad's night continued as expected and everything went smoothly. There weren't any big mishaps and everyone seemed to go away full and happy.

As the night began to draw to an end, his mind began to roam back to the farm and he couldn't help but wonder if things were going as well at the house with his mom and Noelle.

****

Noelle's mom had called back with flight information. She had been fortunate to catch a flight out later that afternoon. She would come into the Indianapolis airport at 6:16 p.m. Angelina and Noelle would be there to pick her up and the plan was that they would come straight back to the farm. Her sisters had made arrangements to go next door to the neighbor's where they both had friends their own age. Genie had promised to call them as soon as she knew anything. She kissed them both and left with a quick hug. As the girls watched her pull away, they began to speculate. What was going on with their big sister? No matter how many times they reviewed the last few weeks, there was no clue as to what was wrong with Noelle. The only option that they had was to wait for the answers to come. However, they made sure that Noelle's phone and charger were packed with their mom so that they would have a way to talk to her.

The girls unpacked their suitcases, put away Anaya's clothes, and got ready to go next door. The doorbell rang as Nissa was begging to wear one of the new shirts that her sister had purchased. Answering it they found their friends from across the street full of questions about what was up and wanting to know why the need to stay at their house. The sisters didn't really have any answers so they just said that they weren't sure what was up. All they knew was that Noelle was having car trouble and that their mother needed to help her out. With that being said they all headed up to check out the new clothes that Anaya had just bought and get ready to go next door.

The girls were going to be careful not to share too much at this point. This was so out of character for their sister that they were not sure what was about to happen. Yet they both felt the need to protect her privacy without even talking to the other one. Tomorrow would bring what it would. However, after the last year, they were not ready to become the center of the gossip ring in their school again.

* * * *

Genie's flight was called to board and she grabbed her overnight bag. She had packed light. Her main objective had been to get to her daughter and get the problem straightened out. She just wanted to wrap Noelle in her arms and make everything all right. Then her next objective was to get her back home.

When she booked her flight, she just booked for a one way ticket. She wasn't sure if they would be flying back yet tonight or tomorrow. Then there was the car that Noelle had mentioned; the car that somehow had trouble. She didn't know if that was serious or if they would be driving that car back. If so, that would be a longer trip back. How her daughter had gotten so far away by herself she couldn't imagine. Then the thought hit her that she was assuming that she was by herself. She didn't really know that did she? Genie's head was beginning to pound with all of the questions that were running through her mind.

When she had called and given Noelle the arrival information, she had a head full of questions that she wanted to ask. She sensed that it would be better to wait until she was face to face with her daughter. That would happen soon. The flight time was 1 hour and 35 minutes. It wouldn't be long before she landed.

Noelle had seemed relieved and yet there was something else in her voice. Genie couldn't put her finger on it; maybe it was a hesitancy. She was certain from Noelle's reaction that her daughter was glad she would be there so quickly. Genie certainly was relieved. She was not sure she could have waited much longer to hold Noelle in her arms and make sure that she was okay. She leaned her head back and closed her eyes to rest as the plane prepared for take off. She did not love to fly. The take offs were always the worst part for her. This one wasn't so bad though. The fatigue of the weekend and the stress of worrying about Noelle had taken its toll on her and the next thing that she remembered was the voice on the loud speaker asking everyone to prepare for landing. They were already there. She had slept through the whole trip and she was finally going to get to see her daughter.

****

Noelle and Angelina had plenty of time to get ready and get to the airport. Noelle was anxious and scared all at the same time. As the overhead speaker announced that her mother's plane had landed and they began to watch for the passengers to disembark, Noelle noticed that her hands were sweaty and her mouth was dry. What was she going to say? What was her mom going to say?

She looked at Angelina with that look of uncertainty. "What next?" Noelle asked her.

"One step at a time and we don't get ahead of God. Remember?" Angelina took a hold of Noelle's hand and squeezed.

At just that moment Genie exited through the terminal and Noelle saw her coming. The two locked eyes and both began to run. They met in the middle. Finally in the arms of her mother, Noelle began to cry. Genie held onto her daughter. For this moment, Noelle wasn't her 19 year old; but the little girl of the past who needed her mother to make everything all right again. Genie resolved then and there to do just that. She would protect her daughter through whatever was to come. A mother cub could not have been more protective.

Angelina hung back and gave them the moment that they both needed. Tears were filling her eyes as she watched from a distance knowing that they too were crying. She could see that Noelle's mom was soothing her daughter. Though she could not hear what was being said, she knew that they were words of love. That was what Noelle needed at this very moment. However, Angelina also knew that they would both need strength to get through the conversation that was going to happen later.

Please God fill their hearts with preparation for what is about to come. Give them both the Wisdom of Solomon to deal with what is going to be said. Lead their conversations, soften their words, and heal the hearts that are going to break in a way that only You can. We love you Father. Amen.

As her prayer ended, she saw Noelle turn her mother toward Angelina and walk that way. Angelina wasn't sure, not knowing Noelle's mother, what to expect. So she was prepared for almost anything. What happened melted her heart.

As they approached the spot where she was standing, Angelina reached out her hand to Genie who took her hand and pulled her into a warm and appreciative embrace. She whispered into her ear, "Thank you so much for taking care of my daughter. I will never be able to thank you enough. There were so many horrible things that could have happened. I will always be grateful."

Angelina hugged her back and with tears said, "It was my pleasure. She is a wonderful girl. You have done a great job. You should be so proud. Now…let's get you guys back to the farm. I'm sure that you're anxious to talk with her. The sooner we get going, the sooner that can happen."

Genie was relieved that this woman understood her need to know what was going on. She also had determined that she would let Noelle take the lead on this conversation. She was not going to push. She was going to be patient. She knew her daughter well enough to know that whatever she was about to tell her wasn't going to be easy for either one of them. This conversation was hard enough for Noelle that she had chosen to run away and she had said earlier that she had done so to protect the family. Genie had begun to prepare herself for what was coming. She was ready to help her…no matter what! They headed to the car. She couldn't take her eyes off of Noelle as she quickly inventoried her daughter making sure that she was okay physically. Relief was flooding over her. Noelle was safe. Nothing else mattered. Whatever it was… would be okay.

CHAPTER 18

PSALM 16:7-11
I will praise the LORD, who counsels me;
even at night my heart instructs me.
I have set the LORD always before me.
Because He is at my right hand, I will not be shaken.
Therefore my heart is glad and my tongue rejoices;
my body also will rest secure,
because You will not abandon me to the grave,
Nor will You let Your Holy One see decay.
You have made known to me the path of life;
You will fill me with joy in Your presence,
with eternal pleasures at your right hand.

THE MOMENT FOR TRUTH

THE RIDE TO THE FARM WAS QUIET. NOELLE LET HER MOM sit in the front seat of the SUV with Angelina and she set in the back seat. That way she could watch her mom and try to read her expressions. Frequently Genie would turn and smile at her. Once she reached back and took hold of and squeezed her hand. Noelle's heart was breaking. She was moments away from delivering to this woman that she adored the worst news possible that a mom could receive. How could she do this?

Angelina kept the conversation flowing so the atmosphere wasn't so threatening. What a God send this woman had become in her life. The ride wasn't long. Within 60 minutes of leaving the airport traffic they were at the driveway to the farm. Noelle was amazed that in such a short period of time, they could go from bumper to bumper traffic to an area that looked remote and so private. They went from a highway to a dirt road. It was as if they had just taken a step back into years gone by.

The vehicle came to a stop in the garage and they all climbed out. Noelle grabbed her mom's overnight bag and slung it over her shoulder. As they followed Angelina into the kitchen, Genie grabbed her daughter's hand and held on as if holding onto a lifeline. Noelle liked the feel of security that it gave her. It was as if her mom was telling her she was going to be okay.

Angelina went immediately into the kitchen and turned on the water to heat hot chocolate. Noelle had told her before they left for the airport that her mom loved to sit in front of a fire and sip chocolate. Knowing that, she had gotten everything ready before they left so that in minutes of coming home they could be comfy in the living room.

"Why don't you let me take your bag upstairs? I thought that maybe the two of you would like to share the room that Noelle has been occupying."

"Thank you very much," Genie said. "My, what a beautiful home you have. It's so much more than just a house. It has such a warm, welcoming feeling to it."

"The Lord has blessed us and that's why I'm always so excited when I'm given the chance to share it. Please make yourselves at home. Noelle knows that what I have is yours for as long as you need it. I'm very happy to be able to help in any way that the Lord allows." Angelina went up the stairs to deposit the bag. Noelle knew that she was disappearing to give mom and daughter time alone without a stranger hovering over them. Yet Noelle longed for the strength that Angelina brought so easily.

Genie wasn't sure how to take all of the talk about the

Lord. She wasn't used to hearing someone so out spoken about their faith. However, she was more grateful than words could express about the safety that had been given to Noelle.

"Mom, do you want to sit here on the couch? I'm sure that you have so many questions. I don't even know where to start."

Genie was full of questions. Instead of asking she said, "Honey, why don't you start wherever you're comfortable. Just know that there isn't anything that you could possibly tell me that's going to change the way that I feel about you. You're my daughter. Nothing else matters. I'm not here to judge you. I'm here to love you."

That being said, Noelle burst into tears and began to apologize. "Mom, I'm so sorry. I've made a mess of everything. This is all my fault. I don't want you to blame yourself. I did this. Not you. I don't want you to feel like you are responsible. You've been the best mom ever."

Her mom wrapped her arms around Noelle and rocked her. Her thoughts went back in time, a time that seemed so long ago, Noelle was little and would climb up onto Genie's lap. They would rock away all of her problems. She wanted to turn back the hands of time for Noelle. She wanted to make everything better.

"There…there. It's going to be all right. You just tell me what's wrong and then we'll work on fixing the problem. Don't make this any harder on yourself then it has already been. Just say the words. Get them out and we'll go from there. You've agonized over this for too long already. You never have to feel like you're in a problem by yourself."

Angelina was in the kitchen now. She was quietly praying, Father, give her the strength to say the words.

"Mom…I…I'm…I'm…" That long pause and Genie could feel Noelle quiver in her arms.

"Just say it Honey." Genie softly whispered to her first

born rocking in her arms.

Noelle took a deep breath, "I'm pregnant". The sobs came harder and faster.

"Oh Honey…Oh my baby girl…It's going to be alright. It's going to be okay. Shshsh." Genie rocked her daughter, stroking her hair. Her tears were falling down her cheeks and onto Noelle's hair.

Angelina stood in the kitchen silently crying and thanking God that the words were out. She continued to pray, Father we need Your presence. We need Your wisdom. We need Your love.

Time seemed to stand still as the two, mother and daughter, held each other. Moments became minutes until there was a quieting and Genie was just staring into the eyes of her oldest daughter. She just wanted to take away the pain and make everything better. She wanted to kiss away the hurt the way that she used to do when Noelle had fallen off her bike or pinched her finger. Only this time she knew that she couldn't kiss away this hurt. She knew that this was the beginning of many hurts to come. She knew that Noelle's life was changing. Genie knew that as a mother, nothing would ever be the same for Noelle again. Regardless of what the future held.

"Mom…I'm so sorry."

"No more being sorry. We're past that. From now on we just have to work together to make sure that you and the baby are safe and healthy. Do you understand what I am saying? I love you! That does not change. I love you. Okay?"

"Okay."

Angelina heard the words that she had longed to hear… 'Make sure that you and the baby are safe.' It had all been worth it; worth all of the pain of reliving the past; worth all of the memories that she had buried from so long ago. It was worth every agonizing moment. This baby would live. This baby would have a future. "Thank you God!" was all that she could say.

This seemed to be the time for the hot chocolate. It would give everyone a moment to collect their thoughts. She carried the tray into the living room and offered the hot cups of chocolate with whipping cream on the top to both Noelle and Genie. "I think that we could use some chocolate." She said.

Genie took a cup and looked into the server's eyes. They exchanged looks that only mothers could understand as she said, "Thank you!"

Angelina replied, "It was my pleasure".

They sat in silence for a few moments watching the fire as they sipped the warm liquid. No one seemed to be in a hurry. The moment that had plagued them was past and now they could relax and take their time with the rest of the story.

When the drinks were gone, Angelina gathered the cups and came back with a box of tissues. Each of them blew their noses. The nervousness of the moment and the noise coming from all three of them at once made them laugh. They say that laughter is good for the soul. Today it certainly was.

"Okay. How about we put the rest of this puzzle together for me?" Her mother suggested. "Like…how did you get a car and where is it now? You said you had trouble. Did you have an accident?" Genie had more questions.

"Where were you going and why would you leave home when you needed us the most?"

"Well", Noelle began, "Let's start with why I left home. I thought that this was my problem and the only way that I could protect you and the girls was to go. I did not want you to have to deal with the mess that I created. We have all had so much to deal with this year. I didn't think that it was fair to you. Plus, I thought that I could protect the girls from having to deal with the fall out." Noelle looked ashamed. "You know what everyone at school would say. I thought about what the girls would have to go through. We already know how cruel people can be. I just wanted to go away and take care of the problem."

Genie looked at her daughter with questions eyes, "By 'take care of the problem' you mean…?"

"I thought that if I went away where you couldn't find me, I would have an abortion. Then when I came back no one would have to know and you and the girls would be better off."

"Oh Baby. You were going to go through all of this by yourself?" Her mother asked.

"Yes!"

"I don't want to invade where you don't want me to go; but, can I ask…what about the father of this baby? Does he know? What were his thoughts about all of this? Honey, I did not even know that you were seeing someone. I don't understand. We've always talked about everything; why not this?" Noelle's mom seemed a little hurt. Her daughter had obviously had a life that she hadn't been sharing.

"Well…I guess that when Dad left I just tried to cover up some of the pain in crazy ways. I went to college and people were having parties. At first I didn't go; but, everyone seemed to be having so much fun and I couldn't stop thinking about Dad leaving and what we had been through. It seemed so unfair. So…I went and there was drinking. It started with just a couple of drinks a night. It seemed harmless. Plus, for a few hours I didn't think about Dad. You never knew. If I came home, you were in bed. By the morning everything was fine." Noelle began to feel the shame sink into her being.

She had started and she wasn't going to stop until the story was all out. She didn't want to carry this with her anymore. So she continued.

"I knew it was wrong. That's why I never brought home any of those kids for you to meet. I didn't want them to have any contact with the girls. I had to protect them from people who made those kinds of choices. I didn't really think about the fact that I was one of those people."

"If I drank too much I would just stay in the dorm. If you were expecting me at home, I would send a text letting you know that I was going to be up late studying with friends and that I would stay at one of their houses. It became so easy to lie. One lie just led to another. You never questioned me. Once I started telling little lies, it became easy to tell bigger ones."

Genie felt a tugging of guilt. "Oh Honey…I'm so sorry. I should have been more aware. It was just that you've never given me cause to question you. You've always been so honest with me that I never would have guessed…I mean…I should have…I don't know…"

"No Mom! This isn't your fault. Please don't go there. After all of this, if you blamed yourself, I'd feel even worse. You've been a wonderful mother. Promise me that you won't ever think those thoughts again. This is my fault. No! You taught me how to make better choices. It was my choice not to do what I knew was best." Noelle lovingly stroked her mom's cheek.

Genie kissed the hand that was comforting her and said, "Okay. I won't go there if you don't."

"So…what about the father?" Genie asked again.

"Well…there was this party…and there was a lot of craziness going on. I didn't know many of the people there. It was a 'by invitation only party' at one of the sorority houses on campus. I went with a couple of girls who I hung around with at school. We were all excited to have been invited. It was our first time. I knew as soon as I got there that it was not a great place to be. But you know…I was there. These were older guys and some of them seemed so nice. Every time my glass emptied, there was someone filling it again." Noelle began to cry as she started reliving the memories of that night.

"I don't know what happened except I began to feel woozy and the next morning I woke up in a bed. The bed was dirty. It was gross. I could hardly open my eyes. My head was pounding and there was pain. You know. Down there". She was crying harder now. "He was there. His back was to me. He was passed out. I didn't even know who it was. I didn't remember going into that room and I don't…" The sobs were coming faster and harder…"I don't remember what happened while I was in there. I just knew that I had to get out of there before anyone saw me and I had to get away from him; whoever he was."

"Oh no! No. No. Oh my Baby." Genie cried as she held her daughter. She felt so many emotions as Noelle's pain ripped her heart in half. How could this have happened to her daughter? This was a nightmare that she should be hearing on the TV or reading in a magazine. This might happen to others girls, but not to one of her girls.

And then she thought, how ironic that after living through the leaving of her husband, I could still think that as a family we were above this kind of happening. Somehow she still believed that they were immune. Her first thought was that she had to get her head out of the sand and start seeing reality.

Taking her daughter by the shoulders and looking deep into her eyes, Genie said, "Noelle…this is not your fault. No one has the right to do something to you without your consent."

"I know that Mom; but, it is my fault. I should not have been there. I should not have been drinking. I put myself in a bad situation that set me up to have bad things happen to me. I was so ashamed. Everything changed for me that night. I was angry. I lost something that I can never get back. I can't go back and be a little girl ever again."

The look on Noelle's face became harder, "It was just another thing that had been ripped away from me. Just like Dad. I became determined that from that moment on I would be in control of my destiny and no one else was ever going to hurt me again. There were no more parties and I became totally focused on my classes."

She continued, "A few weeks later I knew something was wrong. I didn't feel right. At first I could not believe that it would be possible. Then I knew. I bought a pregnancy test and it was positive."

Noelle looked to her mother to see how she was handling all of this information. Genie answered with, "It's okay Honey…we're okay. Go on."

"I began to put together a plan. I began to get things in place so that when the opportunity presented its self, I would be ready. The trip to Aunt Debbie's was exactly what I needed to happen. I wrote the note, bought a car, and waited for you to leave."

"Why here?" Genie asked.

"I didn't even know where here was. I just knew that I wasn't going south because we think that Dad is that way. So I went north. I took back roads so I wouldn't be noticed incase something went wrong and you were looking for me. It took me longer. I didn't follow a map; I just turned when I felt like turning. I was just driving…anywhere. Not even thinking about where."

Noelle continued, "Then on the third day, I had a tire blow on the car and I was stranded just down the road. Angelina's son Brad found me and they have been helping me ever since.

"Mom", Noelle came to the first bright spot in her whole story, "I believe that God directed my path. I could have ended up anywhere; but, He steered me here to the most wonderful family."

Noelle looked at Angelina and asked, "Is it okay if I share your story with my mom?"

"Without hesitating Angelina answered, "Of course Honey. You do whatever you need to do."

"Mom, Angelina had an abortion when she was young. She had never shared that with anyone except her husband before me. I know that God sent me here so that she could give me truth. Because of her story I know that taking the life of this baby would not make my life any easier. I don't know what the answers are or what the future holds; but, I do know that I can't make this story worse by doing something that I'd have to live with for the rest of my life."

"Noelle, I don't know what the answers are at this moment either. I do know that we can figure them out together though." She held her daughter's hand and thought about what to do next.

Angelina spoke, "This has been a lot of information to digest in a short period of time. I'm suggesting that we have some supper and rest on it for the night. Things will look different in the morning. They always do. What do you both think?"

"Angelina, we have already taken up so much of your time. I hate to inconvenience you one moment longer." Genie said as she reached across and squeezed Angelina's hand.

"Nonsense!" Angelina answered immediately. "The first thing that Noelle will tell you is that I love being able to help. Plus, I too believe that this has been an opportunity for me to do some healing. I think that God has given me a gift. He allowed me to use my story to make a difference in the life of this baby. As Noelle told you, I wasn't lucky enough to have anyone direct me away from abortion. It was a horrible part of my life that I will always carry. It's only been through the grace of the Father and the shedding of Jesus' blood on the cross, that I've been able to live with the decision that I made. So it's been my pleasure to be here when God brought Noelle. I feel like my baby's life had a purpose…even though."

With tears in her eyes Genie answered, "In that case, we graciously accept your offer to stay the night. And we both thank you for being willing to be as open as you have been."

Noelle took a hold of Angelina's hand and said, "Could I ask one more think of you?"

"Of course…ask anything." She answered.

"Would you pray with us now? I think it could help us."

Smiling she answered, "I'd love to". Angelina bowed her head and Noelle and Genie followed her lead.

"Most Gracious Father, we are so grateful for Your faithfulness through these days. You have heard our pleas and answered. We continue to seek You for direction on the decisions that will need to be made. Will You prepare the hearts of Noelle's sisters so that they too will be accepting and understanding. Only You know what tomorrow holds. We wait upon Your lead and know that You want only the best for us. Father, protect this unborn child. May he or she be blessed all the days of his or her life? And may Your plan and purpose be brought to fruition. We ask that You bless Genie and Noelle's family with Your grace and mercy all the days of their lives and help them to grow in Your wisdom as they continue to seek You. In Jesus Name. Amen.

Genie wasn't sure that she understood this religion thing. She did know that she was thankful that her daughter had been protected these last days. And if that was Jesus, then maybe she should be open to learning more about Him. However, she did have to wonder, if He really exists, where was He when she was at the party and why wasn't He protecting her then? Those were questions for another day though. Today she would just be grateful for the opportunity to wrap her arms around her daughter and hold her close. She did agree that they would let tomorrow bring what it would.

After a wonderful bite to eat and again telling Angelina thank you, Noelle and Genie retired to the bedroom. There they talked about the girls and Genie felt like they should tell them in person. For tonight, Noelle took her phone that the girls had packed and called them herself. She apologized for causing them concern and promised that she was okay. Not wanting to get into a deep discussion with their friends present, their answer to her was that they loved her and would talk about it when she got home. They all said good night.

As they lay in bed, Noelle filled in the spaces that were left out of the telling of her story. She especially enjoyed telling about how she had seen a personal God at work in her life. They talked for hours until finally drifting off to sleep.

Noelle's last words were, "Angelina has been teaching me not to get ahead of God. So I'm trying to give Him the lead in my life."

Genie's last thoughts were concerns for her daughter and the decisions that were still to be made.

CHAPTER 19

PSALM 4:6-8
Many are asking, "Who can show us any good?"
Let the light of your face shine upon us O LORD.
You have filled my heart with greater joy
than when their grain and new wine abound.
I will lie down and sleep in peace,
for You alone, O LORD, make me dwell in safety.

PEACE IN THE MORNING

NOELLE WOKE WITH THE SAME CONFUSION THAT SHE WOKE up with the morning before. It took her a few minutes to remember. When she did, she immediately rolled over to see her mother watching her.

Her smile tentative, she asked, "Is everything okay?"

"Good morning Sweetheart. I was just enjoying watching you sleep and thinking about those mornings when you were a little girl and for whatever reason you would come to my bed in the middle of the night and I would take you in my arms and snuggle with you. Even then I knew that all too soon those days would be over and no more would you need me to make everything better."

"Oh Mom…I need you more than you could possibly know. Look at what a mess I've made."

"No Honey. You didn't cause this problem by yourself. Your dad and I helped you. And though it's admirable of you to want to take responsibility for all of this, it isn't fair to look past the part that we played. We too will have to take the responsibility that belongs to us; just as you'll have to take responsibility for your part."

"Dad is never going to know. And after what he did, he certainly isn't going to feel responsible for any of this."

"Well…I guess that we can't worry about what he is going to do or not going to do. We can only be responsible for us. Isn't that what we've learned this year. You know what?"

"What?"

"I think that we've been a pretty good team…the four of us. We'll walk together through this just as well."

"Her mother continued, "You'll never know how proud I am of you and your need to handle all of this by yourself. What a strength I see in you. These are some of the hardest days that you'll face. Yet, you're taking responsibility and going forward. I wasn't much older than you are now when my life was mapped out for me. I would marry your dad, we would have a wonderful family, he would take care of us, and we would live happily ever after. Maybe if I had been more involved in the planning of our life, I would have seen the future coming. I was so trusting that it was easy for him to cover it all up and leave us. I'm envious that even in adversity you could take charge and move ahead…even if it was in the wrong direction…you weren't afraid to do what you thought necessary."

"Mom…don't think that I wasn't afraid. I was just more worried about protecting all of you than I was of the fear inside of me."

"Honey, I hope that you understand now that you're not alone. Whatever the future holds, we'll be right there walking through it together."

Noelle snuggled in close to her mom. "I wish that I could crawl into your bed and you could make all of this go away. I wish I could be that little girl again. I don't want to have to make such hard decisions now."

Genie loved the feel of Noelle in her arms and she wanted to stay that way forever. She wanted to protect her daughter from what lay ahead; but she knew that she could only be there with her. She could not make the problems go away.

"Honey, I have to ask a question." She ventured.

"It's okay Mom. Ask whatever you want. I don't have very many answers though."

"It's about what happened to you that night. Have you wondered about pressing charges or at least talking to the police? I mean what about other girls who may fall into the same assault? You do realize that what happened to you is a crime? It isn't okay for them to do what they did."

Noelle hesitated for a moment, "I have thought about it over and over. That would mean bringing all of the ugliness of that night out into the open. It would mean that I would have to share with others what I did and what was done to me. It isn't something that I'm proud of. My name could be broadcast across the TV. People at school would know about the freshman girl and what happened to her. I'd be judged by people who don't even know me." Noelle shivered at the thought.

She continued, "I don't know if I'm strong enough to do that. Plus, I'll be pregnant. There would be paternity testing and what if I decide to give the baby up for adoption and the boy's family doesn't want to do that. I just don't know what the best thing is for the baby at this point. I mean that really is what I have to think about now. Isn't it?"

Genie realized that her daughter had given great thought to these things. She also realized that these were not her decisions to make. The decisions, as hard as they were going to be, were Noelle's.

Noelle knew that she had to share all that was on her mind, "Mom, I'm not sure that I want to go back home. I mean…

maybe it would be better for me to have the baby away from where people know me. That way whatever decision I make, I don't have to explain to anyone. Life just goes on. That way Nissa and Anaya don't have to deal with any consequences of this."

"Oh Honey…I don't know. I want to be with you. I want to take care of you and be there for you. I think that the girls will feel that way too. We love you. You're a part of us. Without you our team is broken and we're incomplete."

"I know. But stop and think about what the girls have already been through with Dad and the way everyone talked. It made a huge impact on the choices that I made. More than I realized. But, now that I know, I want to protect them as much as I can."

Genie frowned, "Maybe I should have insisted on counseling for all of us. It might have made a difference."

"We can't second guess what's past; however, we can learn from it. I don't think that it would be a bad idea to let the girls talk with someone who could help them sort through some of their feelings. At the time I didn't think that I needed it. Now I know those feelings affected the choices that I made." She continued.

"Mom…don't blame yourself. We all did the best under the circumstances. It wasn't something that we could prepare for. I've seen a difference between the way that Angelina's family approaches things. They seem to have more of a peace in their lives. God certainly seems to have made a difference. He is very real to them in everything. I'm thinking that it wouldn't hurt to try and find a little of the peace that they've found."

"Oh Noelle, I don't know. I haven't ever understood the need for corporate religion. Those were some of the same people who made us feel the worst when your father left.

"I know. I didn't say that I had any answers. I just wish

that I could find some of what Angelina and Brad have. It certainly works for them."

"We'll see. Who knows what we'll find when we start looking for answers. Speaking of which…we better start getting around or Angelina will think that we're lazy house guest. Genie hugged her daughter one more time and they both started getting ready for the day ahead of them.

Before leaving the room, Noelle called her sisters to check on them. They were getting ready for school. She didn't get into any deep conversation. She just let them know that she was missing them and that she loved them. When they asked if she would be home today, she said she didn't think so; but they would talk later after school.

Noelle felt sadness come over her when she hung up. She really was beginning to realize that nothing was going to be the same ever again.

They both took quick showers and headed down the stairs and into the kitchen where they found Angelina and Brad. They were sitting at the bar having breakfast.

Mornings at the Conroy's home were amazing. The smells, the atmosphere, the fellowship all blended together to create such a warm and welcoming start to the day. Noelle loved the coziness of sitting around the bar in the middle of the kitchen where Angelina created art. It was so much more than food; it truly was a work of art; Angelina's own unique touch. She made you feel so special.

"Good morning." Angelina and Brad chimed.

"Good morning." They answered back.

"Come and sit with us." Angelina motioned as she turned to the oven and whisked out two covered plates which she sat in front of the two women.

As Noelle took the seat next to Brad, Angelina made introductions. "Genie, this is my oldest son, Brad. Bradley this is Noelle's mother, Genie Smith."

"It's a pleasure to have you with us Mrs. Smith. I hope you have some time to check out the farm while you're here. I'd love to show the two of you around this afternoon. I am quite proud of our facilities. It isn't large but it's been built by the hands of my father and now I'm continuing. We don't have a lot of livestock. We have invested more time into crop farming. However, the eggs that you're going to eat today are from our own chickens; range fed with no preservatives. I guarantee that they will be the best you've ever eaten. Of course it helps that Mom is the best cook for miles around."

"Thank you for the offer Brad. And please call me Genie." She said. "A tour would be very nice. However at this point we don't know what our plans are. I understand that Noelle has a car with some problems that we are going to have to attend to. Then we have to make some decisions about returning home."

"Well don't worry about the car. I took care of that yesterday. There is a new tire already mounted and back on her car. It's sitting in the driveway ready for whenever it's needed." Brad said.

"Brad, thank you again for all that you've done. What do I owe you for that tire?" Noelle asked.

Brad smiled at Noelle and said, "There's a bill from the station in the car. A friend of the family owns the station and he brought me the tire yesterday while I was at the restaurant. I'd have paid for it; but, he wouldn't take my money. Just handed me the bill and said to drop it off when I was back in town."

"Oh…that was so kind. I'll take care of it right after breakfast. I'll leave the money on the bar, if that's alright." Noelle smiled her reply.

Brad could feel that crazy heat rising up in him again. "That's fine. I'm in and out of town often during the course of a week. But for now, I have to be off to class. I hope that you ladies have a wonderful morning. I'll be back sometime after 1:00. Hope to see you then." With that he kissed his mom on the cheek, grabbed a back pack and coat, and walked out the door.

Noelle heard the truck start and there was a loneliness that followed. She liked the feeling of Brad's presence. There was a protective spirit that just seemed to be around him. It was a good feeling. There was strength in him that just made you feel safe. Instantly her mind remembered why she was here and the place that she was now would live. She thought to herself, "If only things were different." But…they weren't and she had to look to the future.

Angelina removed the covers off the plates and in front of the girls was the most scrumptious looking breakfast. A Belgium waffle covered in a fruity sauce of strawberries and what smelled like real maple syrup. Before they could speak Angelina took real whipped cream and put a dollop on both waffles. As if that wasn't enough, there were two eggs over medium and two pieces of sausage.

Angelina said, "God bless this food and the people who eat it. Amen. Genie, are you a coffee drinker. I have a fresh pot made." Angelina offered.

"Oh…I would love a cup of coffee. I limit myself to one cup a day. It's my morning wake up. Black would be great. Angelina you shouldn't have gone to all of this trouble. This looks amazing; and smells almost too good to eat. Thank you."

"No trouble. I love to do this."

"Mom, I have said 'thank you' so many times since arriving here. Angelina and Brad have gone out of there way to make me feel welcome. I have been taken care of so well. I feel so blessed."

Genie looked at Angelina with her mother eyes. Angelina nodded letting her know that she understood. She reached across and took the hand of the woman that had protected her daughter and said, "No…we have been so blessed. Thank you Angelina."

"Seriously…you two; I haven't done anything that I don't love to do. If you feel welcomed in our home then we have only done what God calls us to do. I'm glad for the opportunity to walk in His ways."

There was that churchy stuff again. Genie wasn't sure about all of that. It confused her. She was not used to someone talking so openly about God and his ways. She had to admit that it made her feel a little uncomfortable. She did notice how easily it came for Angelina to talk about God though. Maybe she would have to ponder on that some. Maybe Noelle was right; could they, as a family, have missed something all of these years by not pursuing religion more?

Not religion. Pursue me.

Genie paused. She was not sure where that thought came from. She hadn't really heard it. Or had she? Maybe she had just thought it. Although, it didn't really sound like something that she would have thought.

Angelina said, "Eat girls while it's still warm; enjoy all of those yummy calories".

They all laughed and while they ate the girls chattered away about the life here. Angelina told them about her two boys and the difference between them. She told about her husband dying and how she and the boys continued to build their lives on a day to day basis standing on the foundation that God had supplied.

Genie marveled at the peace that she too could feel; the peace that Noelle had also sensed. She wondered how you find something that can sustain you the way that this family seems to have found their strength.

She had seen church at work. This wasn't like anything that she had ever experienced. No one that she knew lived a life so sure of a God. Not like Angelina did. It did not make sense to her. How do you depend on someone that you can't even see. She always thought that church was just some place to go and get a nice, warm, fuzzy feeling; a place where a pastor performs marriage ceremonies. A place that you call when someone you love dies. She had always wanted the surety of belonging to an organization in case she ever needed to purchase their services. She just didn't want to be dictated to by their ideas. Some of it seemed too out there; too strange for her liking. Still…it did seem to work for these people. And they had certainly been wonderful. She was beginning to understand why Noelle was questioning if things could have been different in their family.

Noelle broke into her train of thought. "Mom, where did you go?"

"O sorry Honey. I was just thinking. We're going to have to make some decisions."

CHAPTER 20

PSALM 119:35-39
Direct me in the path of your commands,
for there I find delight.
Turn my heart toward Your statues
and not toward selfish gain.
Turn my eyes away from worthless things;
preserve my life according to Your word.
Fulfill Your promise to Your servant,
so that You may be feared.
Take away the disgrace I dread,
For Your laws are good.

EVERYONE NEEDS A PLAN

"WOULD THE TWO OF YOU LIKE ME TO LEAVE SO THAT you can work through this together? I certainly understand that you would need some time alone." Angelina offered.

"No…please stay." Noelle answered without hesitation. "You've been so helpful."

"Angelina, Noelle is right. You bring such calm to the problem. We would both appreciate any assistance that you could offer. Of course, that is…if you don't mind. We have already taken up so much of your time." Genie was sincere as she tilted her head and sent Angelina a warm, apologetic smile.

"If I can help in anyway, I would love to. However, you have to promise me that if you feel like I'm pushing, you'll say so. I have such a tendency to take charge. I'm afraid I'm a control freak to a fault."

The girls laughed. Noelle looked at her mom and raised her two fingers on her right hand. She waited until Genie followed suit and in a sing song voice they both said, "We promise."

They helped Angelina take care of the breakfast dishes and then settled into the living area in front of the fire again. It was becoming their favorite spot to talk. It was so comforting and non-threatening. There was a warmth to the room that made you feel at ease; even in the midst of struggle.

Genie looked at Noelle and said, "So where do we start? We're going to have to make some decisions about going back home. I know you said that you're thinking about staying in this town; but as your mom, I'm not considering that idea at all."

"Mom, we have to face it, my life is going to change in the next few months."

"That's exactly why I need you to be home where the girls and I can help."

"Let's talk about the girls. You know how it was when Dad left. The whole school was buzzing. We couldn't even go into town without people staring. I got so sick of those looks of pity. And you knew what they were thinking. Well… now I've created another situation to give them something to buzz about. And I don't care what they'll say about me. I just don't want the girls to have to go through that again. We've talked about how hard that time was for all of us. I know they will agree with me. The talk was the worst part of what we went through. I can't put them through more of that."

Genie felt the need to explain what they were referring to so that Angelina would understand. So she told her quickly about the girls' father just leaving without even saying good-bye. "He left us a letter telling us that he was sorry. He said that he had found someone new and that he had to start over with this woman. We never knew who she was and we have never talked with my husband again. He set up everything to be handled through an attorney. He left us financially comfortable and alone. It was a shock to say the least. This was totally out of character for him. We all seemed to be very happy including Gale, who was my husband and the girls' father. We were married twenty-two years and I could count on one hand the times that we disagreed about anything. Our lives changed direction with one letter. That was a year ago. We're learning how to survive."

Angelina could feel the sorrow that held their family captive. She said, "I'm sorry. I can see that the wound is still very fresh and painful. If he wasn't a selfish man, then he must also be very broken knowing the pain that he has caused all of you. It cannot be easy for anyone involved living with the devastation that his decisions caused."

Genie was taken back by the words that Angelina spoke. She had never given Gale's feelings a thought during this time. Why should she? He hadn't thought about theirs. He hadn't thought about what this was going to do to them. Had he?

"Why would you say that? What would make you think about his feelings?" Genie asked.

"I don't know. I hope that doesn't offend you? I guess that I was just thinking that if this was a man that seemed to love his family for twenty-two years, then he must have. He couldn't have been pretending for all of that time. It just seems like he left with no way to find closure ever, which means that he will have to live with the guilt of his actions. It appears almost as if he put in place his own punishment." Angelina knew that she was walking on touchy ground. She hoped that she was not overstepping her boundaries.

"I have to admit; I've never thought about what happened

from the perspective of what he was living with. I've only seen this as something that happened to the girls and myself. To be honest with you, I don't know that I want to think about what he's living with. I've survived this year by trying to build up a hatred for him. It seemed easier to go on that way. I certainly have not wanted to humanize him.

Genie looked at her daughter sitting beside her on the couch. She wondered what Noelle was thinking.

Noelle shrugged her shoulders and said, "Wow. I have to say that I haven't thought about it that way either. Maybe we need to, to help ourselves. I don't think that I'm ready to want to help him. But it certainly hasn't helped me to carry all of this anger towards him."

"We can face a problem head on and depending on how we do it, it can still destroy us. Harboring feelings of hatred and unforgiveness will only be self-destructive. In the end we're hurting ourselves more than we were hurt by the original wound." Angelina offered with an unsure smile.

Genie nodded and said, "I get what you're saying. I'm just not sure that I could go there yet; food for thought." Turning to Noelle she said, "Right now I need to think about you."

Genie continued, "I understand what you're saying about the town and the girls. But what about you; you are not in this alone. As family we can survive anything."

"I know that. Even though I didn't act like I did. You know what I mean…leaving and all. I guess that I just let my emotions take over. I just wanted to protect all of you. That hasn't changed. I still want to protect you. I don't want you to deal with the fallout of my choices." Noelle squared her shoulders. "Mom…that's very important to me."

Genie knew that look; she had seen it over the years when her daughter became determined. She proceeded with caution, not wanting to make this situation combative, "Yes…I get that. But, tell me your plan. Tell me something that will make me feel comfortable leaving you, my pregnant daughter, alone in a place that I don't even know."

"I don't have a plan yet. But, I'm beginning to understand that God does."

"Well…I'm not there yet. I don't even understand what that means. So that isn't good enough for me right now. I need to know that you are safe and comfortable. It is important for me to know that you're not alone; and just as important for me that you are not just physically safe but also emotionally safe." Genie squared her shoulders as stubbornly as her daughter had just done; making it easy to see where Noelle gets that stubborn streak from.

Angelina decided now would be the time to interject. "If I may…perhaps now would be a good time for some insight from an outsider; someone who isn't as personally connected."

"Great!" Both of the women on the couch said at the same time. That breaking the air…they all bcgan to laugh.

Angelina began, "Noelle, if I am understanding you correctly, when you left home you did so to keep your mom and sisters out of the scrutiny of those who would ridicule or pity. Correct?"

"Correct."

"Okay, I understand that from what you've said. But as a mother I also know that it is important that your mom know you are safe, especially now that you are going to go through changes. She's going to want to be a part of all of that. You're going to understand these protective desires as you feel that baby moving and becoming a real part of your life. I'm going to step out on a limb here and feel free to tell me to stop if you want to. Okay?"

"Okaaaaay." Noelle puzzled at where Angelina was going.

"Noelle I think that you and I could agree that we have seen the hand of God in the last few days. I believe that He brought you here for a reason. It just makes sense to me if this is where He wanted you to be for a period of time, that we should accommodate God. That being said, I would like to offer my home to you for as long as you and your family see the need."

Immediately the two women began to protest. Their words all blended together and yet everyone knew what was being said.

"Now stop objecting and let's look at the facts. Not forgetting that God has master minded your travels." Angelina continued. I have a huge home, I have a restaurant where I just lost one of my best workers for an indefinite period of time, and I have a safe area where your family would be welcome to visit as often as possible. What could be more perfect that would meet all the needs of everyone involved including myself? This isn't charity…you need a job and I need a worker."

Silence filled the room.

Angelina stood, "Now, I'm going to go upstairs and give the two of you a chance to mull this over. Call me when you're ready." And she started to leave.

"Wait! Before you go, will you pray with us? There are so many things to consider. I don't want to make the wrong decision. I want God to be pleased." Noelle looked a little teary.

Angelina's heart was so touched. She could see that she was watching a new creature develop before her eyes. Silently she said, "Thank you God!"

Reaching her hands out to the scared ones in front of her Angelina got down on her knees. Genie and Noelle followed suit. "Dear Father, You are so merciful and loving. You know our needs before we do and you always have a fix for us just waiting. We are Your daughters. Be the daddy that each one of us needs. Love us as only You can. Father we ask for Your direction in making the choices that have to be made. We are asking that You love us enough to show us Your way. We don't want to step out in front of You. We are just asking to walk beside of You. Speak clearly to Noelle and Genie. Your will be done. Amen."

That being said, she stood and walked to the stairs and shortly they heard her close the upstairs door.

Sitting back onto the couch, Genie and Noelle just sat staring at each other. Neither one of them knew what to say. They were quietly absorbing their thoughts as they raced through their heads.

From Noelle's perspective she had felt very comfortable in this home from the very beginning. But was comfort what she needed? She realized that there would be nothing comfortable about being a single, pregnant woman. She was going to have to prepare for whatever was to come. In this town she didn't know anyone. There was no one to ask questions and no explanations were necessary. The home came with a job and she needed one.

Genie's mind stumbled over what was best for her daughter, what was best for the girls at home, and what was best for her. She was beginning to understand that Noelle had not dealt with losing her father. Even though on the outside it appeared that she had. Did that also mean that the other girls hadn't? Maybe there were needs at home that she was going to have to begin to address. And if that was so, would it make it harder having Noelle gone from the home or would it be easier for her sisters if they didn't have to deal with the gossip of others?

Noelle spoke first, "Mom, this is so hard. I want to do what is best for everyone. I've watched God at work in all of this. I didn't even know it was Him in the beginning. I think that I'm beginning to recognize His hand in my life a little; enough to know that I want to know more. I still feel strongly that I can't come back home. Staying here, at least for a short while, would be a safe option."

"Oh Honey…I don't know. Angelina and her family have been so wonderful in all of this. I don't want to inconvenience her more. Yet, to have you so far away would be terrifying for me. So staying here and knowing that you were safe would help me get by. After listening to you, I'm wondering if there are sores that I have to open up with the girls so that they can heal. And you; what about your sores?"

"Mom, I think that through this we're finding out that we all have wounds including you. Maybe we tried to be too strong. You loved us so much that your protective hand made it look easy so that our lives could go on. Don't think that you made wrong decisions. At the time we were all just trying to figure out how to survive. I'm not going to blame Dad for where I'm at; but I am realizing that his leaving changed who I was and how I thought. I don't want my sisters to walk the same path that I walked." Noelle started to cry. "Mom, I'm so sorry."

"Shshshshsh. We are going to get through this, you, the girls, and me. We are all going to be just fine.

"I know. There are just so many things that we haven't even discussed. What will I do when the baby is born? Will I keep the baby? Will I put the baby up for adoption? If I do that, can I live with that choice for the rest of my life? Mom how do I figure all of this out by myself?"

Genie realized the weight that was pressing down on her daughter's shoulders. She said the first thing that came to mind, even if she wasn't sure that she believed it. "Honey, you believe that God is directing your path; right? Do you think that He will continue to do that? He hasn't led you in a bad direction so far has He?"

Noelle was encouraged by those words. She also could hear Angelina saying, "Let's not get ahead of God".

"How about this; why don't I go home with you so that we can talk to the girls together? Then I could fly back out here and we could try this for a while and see if this is where God wants me to be? I'll work at the restaurant and save as much money as I can. We will talk everyday. Maybe I could come home for Spring Break." Noelle looked for a reaction from her mother.

As the tears began to build in her eyes, she grabbed her daughter and hung on for dear life. She didn't know how she was going to survive with Noelle's life changing so drastically and hundreds of miles separating them. But she said, "Okay…we'll try it."

CHAPTER 21

PSALM 13:3-6
Look on me and answer, O LORD my God
Give light to my eyes, or I will sleep in death;
my enemy will say, "I have overcome him,"
and my foes will rejoice when I fall.
But I trust in Your unfailing love;
my heart rejoices in Your salvation.
I will sing to the LORD,
for He has been good to me.

WALKING IN TRUST

THE REST OF THE MORNING HAD GONE VERY QUICKLY AFTER Noelle and her mother had made the decision. Sharing with Angelina and then arranging transportation back home. The best flight that they could get had them leaving early the next morning.

Angelina decided that she would go into the restaurant and leave the two of them to spend the afternoon together. Genie didn't say so; but she was glad to have the time alone with her daughter. They asked for directions to town and said that they were going to drive around and look at the area. It was agreed that they would stop at the restaurant for dinner.

Noelle drove and Genie was quite impressed with the little car that Noelle had purchased. She heard how Noelle had made all of the arrangements and put her plan into action to leave without being found. It actually alarmed Genie to know that she could be so thorough about running away.

"Noelle, please promise me that you will never do anything like this again. The world is a scary place and bad things happen to good people." As soon as the words were out of her mouth, Genie realized what she had said. After all…something bad had happened to her daughter with just a few careless choices that seemed harmless at the time.

"I know Mom…believe me…I know."

"I'm sorry. That was insensitive. I didn't mean it that way. I just…wasn't thinking." Her mother apologized.

However it did open the door to some further conversation.

"Noelle…I just keep thinking that there is a father to this baby. I mean…what if he knew that he had fathered a child and wanted to be a part of the baby's life?" Her mother broached the subject carefully.

"I don't even know him. And what he did is criminal. You said yourself that I could press charges. Would it be better for a baby to know his father, if that child was conceived in a rape situation? Mom, this was my first time being with a man. And I don't even remember any of it. Which may be a blessing? I was not planning for something like this. I wasn't on birth control. I didn't go to that party with protection and obviously he didn't either. I don't know if this is a common practice. I've never talked with anyone about what happened."

"It's true. This was a crime and you could press charges. Maybe you should revisit that thought." Genie ventured.

"I could if I wanted my name plastered all over the papers and on the news. Mom, I would just die. You can imagine what they would say about me. Isn't it always the girl's fault?" They were quiet for awhile as Genie considered what her daughter had said.

"That may be what happens; but it is a terrible stigma that doesn't allow any protection for the girl that has been violated." Genie answered.

Noelle, looking at her mother spoke softly yet passionately, "The worst part would be that Dad might see in the news what was going on".

Genie looked straight into her daughter's soul. "And that would be horrible because?"

"Because he might not even care. If he didn't contact me, somehow that would be even worse. I don't want to live with that forever."

If this had done nothing more than open Genie's eyes to the wounds that her daughters were carrying, it had done that. She was beginning to realize that the brokenness was much deeper than they had said. Living with the loss of their father was more than just surviving day after day. She would find a way for them to heal…not just survive.

Genie let that conversation go and began to ask questions about medical attention for Noelle and the baby. She found out that Noelle had gone to the health clinic on campus and they had confirmed the pregnancy. Then they had drawn preliminary blood work, said everything looked good, and gave her a prenatal vitamin to take. She was supposed to follow up with an OB-GYN.

"Have you been taking the vitamins?"

"Yes. Does it seem odd to you that I would do that even while I was making plans to have an abortion?" Noelle asked her mother.

"I think that deep down inside you knew that life is valuable. I don't believe that you would have been able to go through with aborting your baby. If you believe that God has been guiding you through all of this, then you must believe that He has an amazing plan for the two of you."

Noelle looked at her mom and questioned, "For the two of us together…or the two of us separately?"

Genie looked at her daughter and shrugged knowing that Noelle was going to have to make that tough decision; a decision that she would have to live with forever.

Noelle reached for her mother's hand and squeezing it she said, "Thanks Mom…for everything".

Genie nodded, "We're all going to be okay".

The conversation became lighter and they enjoyed their time together. As that time slipped away it became more and more precious to Genie. She knew that with every tick of the clock brought them closer to the time when they would be separated. She was not ready to say good-bye. She wondered, would she ever be able to do that?

****

Brad came home from his classes and found the house empty. Another day that he had anticipated spending some time with this girl and it appeared that it wasn't going to happen. Again there was that feeling of disappointment. He wondered why. She was a total stranger to him. And yet… it seemed to matter. These were such new feelings for him.

There was a note on the bar with cash for the tire. He opened the folded sheet of paper and look at the delicate writing. He remembered noticing how tiny her fingers were. He had even wondered what they would feel like intertwined between his own fingers. His mind wandered as he thought about what it would feel like to hold that small hand in his big hand. He again felt this protective emotion welling up inside of him. How strange these thoughts were. He brought his focus back to the letter.

Dear Brad:
Thank you so much for all that you
have done to help me. You will never know
how much I now appreciate your persistence
that first day. I do believe that God has
directed my path to you and your family. I
look forward to spending more time with all

of you.
Here is the money for the tire. You
have been wonderful. I hope we can talk soon.
Sincerely,

Noelle

Brad reread the note several times. He still was completely in the dark about what was going on. What did she mean by 'spending more time with'? Did that mean that she was going to be staying here in Hadley? He understood why his mom felt like it wasn't her place to tell him what was going on with Noelle; but, he would feel better if he knew something. *Wow...Okay Lord. You are going to have to help me with some patience here. Thanks.*

Brad had chores that he needed to do on the farm and those were his plan for the afternoon. However, he was going into the restaurant for supper and see if he could gather any information from his mom. He assumed that she was there since everyone and all the cars were gone. She should at least be able to shed some light on the 'spending more time' part.

With that Brad grabbed lunch, changed clothes, and headed to the barn.

CHAPTER 22

PSALM 18:28-32
You, O LORD, keep my lamp burning;
my God turns my darkness into light.
With Your help I can advance against a troop;
with my God I can scale a wall.
as for God, His way is perfect,
the Word of the LORD is flawless.
He is a shield for all who take refuge in Him.
For who is God besides the LORD?
And who is the Rock except our God?
It is God who arms me with strength
and makes my way perfect.

COMING OUT OF DARKNESS

BY THE WAY THAT THE EVENING CROWD WAS STARTING, Angelina was glad that she had been able to be here. She had a great staff of employees; even so, she likes to keep her fingers in the mix of everything. She had gotten there early enough to get all of the desserts made and had even had time to place some orders for the next week. Still on her mind was always Noelle. There was no doubt that she had done what God had wanted. Yet, she had done so without even having consulted Brad and Eyan. What were they going to say? Were they going to think it odd that she had offered their home to a complete stranger; a stranger that had a very uncertain future ahead of her? She didn't want to step on Noelle's toes; however, she did feel like the boys should be told what was going on and why. She would talk to Noelle about that conversation soon.

About 6:30 p.m. Noelle and her mother found their way into the restaurant. Why would they be surprised at what they saw? Angelina's restaurant, "Home Away From Home", was so perfectly like her. You couldn't help but feel the love that had gone into creating the atmosphere as soon as you walked into the door. Even the decorations said, "I'm glad that you're here."

They were greeted at the door by a bubbly young woman maybe a little older than Noelle who made them feel like they had been expected.

"Hi. It's so nice to have you with us tonight. My name is Michelle and I'll be your hostess. Would you like to sit in the blue room by the fireplace? I have a nice table available there."

Genie answered with a smile, "That would be lovely Michelle. Thank you."

"Right this way."

They followed Michelle into a dimly lit room with a blazing gas fireplace. Their table was positioned in the corner giving them privacy and a complete view of the room. Gas sconces on the wall gave off just the right amount of light. The table centerpieces were warm and welcoming. This was a place where you could relax from the trials of a hard day and be waited on; a place that you would be drawn to.

Michelle smiled at them and offered, "Could I get you something to drink, coffee, tea, pop or we have a special spiced cider tonight; a warm treat to take the chill off?"

Both of them agreed right away that the cider would be wonderful. Michelle hurried off to get their drinks as they looked around and began to peruse the menu.

"Oh my goodness!" Genie exclaimed. "How could you ever decide what to eat? Everything sounds amazing."

"I've had enough of Angelina's cooking to know that it doesn't matter what you choose; it's all going to be great."

Michelle came back quickly with steaming cups of cider. "Be careful, these are hot. Your waiter will be Shawn. Can I get you anything else while you wait?"

"No thank you, Michelle, you have been most gracious. And we're in no hurry." Genie answered.

While they were trying to decide what to try for dinner, they saw Angelina walking through the rooms. She stopped and talked with everyone. She really was filled with the gift of hospitality. You could just see the faces light up as she stopped and chatted. At one point she stopped to talk with an elderly man and soon they saw her take his hand in hers and she knelt beside his chair, bowed her head, and began to pray with him.

Genie was so touched. She had never seen anyone live out a life of faith the way that Angelina did. It came so natural for her. She was beginning to understand why Noelle was wondering about the choices that they as a family had made. Would her family still be intact if they had made more of an effort to make God the center? There certainly was joy that seemed to surround this whole family; or at least Angelina and Brad. They still had not met Eyan.

Angelina finally made her way to their table. She hugged both of them and said, "Welcome to my 'Home Away From Home'...literally".

"Angelina, it's beautiful; both in the physical and the spiritual. The feeling of peace here is contagious. I'm sure that you have a large group of regulars. And did I see that you were praying with that man?" Genie asked.

"Yes. That happens here often. Mr. Burk just had to place his wife in a nursing home. The poor soul has dementia so bad that it became impossible for him to continue taking care of her. He has done a great job for the last 6 years. Placing her there was so very hard on him. He usually has his meals with her. Tonight she wasn't up to eating so he came here after tucking her into bed for the night. We used to serve them often; now we only see him about once a week. He doesn't like to leave her alone much. What a sad disease."

"Noelle, before you leave tonight, I'll give you a tour; we have several rooms all with a different feel to them. We try to cater to all needs. One of our rooms is very comfortable for someone who has just come straight from a dirty, grimy day of work on the job. As a servant, I want everyone to feel like they have a place. My desire is to meet the needs of whoever walks in that door."

Genie was amazed that there really was someone in this world that was walking the walk of a Christian. You could see it in this family's life at home and at work. And her daughter had basically been dropped into their arms. Maybe this was exactly where Noelle needed to be. Maybe this was where my whole family needs to be? Where did that thought come from? She wondered.

* * * *

Brad got to the restaurant just as the dinner crowd was starting to slow down. After greeting Michelle he asked if there were a couple of new ladies still dining here and was told that they were in the Blue Room. He headed that way saying "Hi" to everyone along the way.

They saw him first and waved.

"Well I see that you've already eaten. I was hoping to join you so that I didn't have to eat alone. You can hardly get Mom to stop and eat when she's working." He said as he sat down.

"Actually, we were just letting our meal settle in hopes of having a piece of your mother's wonderful pie. Mom had roast beef and I went Italian. It was unbelievable and we ate every bite. Now we're so full we aren't sure that we have room." Noelle laughed.

"Oh yah; people come from miles around and have for years just to get Mom's pie."

"This place is wonderful. I've just been watching people. Your mom has created a healing area not just a restaurant. She feeds their soul at the same time that she feeds them physically. And she makes it seem effortless." Genie was in awe.

"That's Mom. She has more energy than an army of people. She can manage the whole kitchen at the same time that she's making sure that everyone's needs are being met out here. Sometimes she'll tell you that she's exhausted; yet you can't see it in her. She always finds more energy and something else that needs to be done. Her staff would move mountains for her. She makes them feel as special as she does the customers. Everyone here really is more like family than employees. Each has come with their own broken stories. God just keeps dropping people who need to be loved on into her life; and she just loves. Have you had a chance to meet anyone from here yet?"

Noelle answered, "Michelle and Shawn".

"Oh…Shawn; he's quite the character. He's as hot tempered as he is funny. The red hair is a dead give away; as Irish as they come. Plus, he would lay down his life for my mom. He walked in here one day a broken mess. She gave him a chance to put his life back together when others wouldn't give him the time of day. He believes that mom is his guardian angel. Now we couldn't get rid of him if we tried. He is glued right to her." Brad laughed. "Here comes the crazy guy now."

"Well…it looks like the sheep came home another day. It's Brad Conroy as I live and breathe." Shawn laughed as he shook Brad's hand.

Brad stood and drew him into a big, bear hug. The two patted each other's backs for a brief moment. You could tell there was a special bond between them.

"You bet and if you weren't such a slacker you could have seen me yesterday. I worked for mom. You were off having a play day." Brad joked.

"That's right. Your Mom works me to the bone." Shawn gave him an expression that showed he was not serious at all.

"How is your brother?" Brad asked.

"Hanging in there, I felt like yesterday I was actually getting somewhere with that stubborn streak in him. He took my advice and started going to one of the Bible Studies that the Chaplin offers. I think that he was at least listening. He asked me some good questions. I was pleased. It was better than going and listening to his anger; all in all a good visit. Keep praying for him. We have a long way to go."

"Too much like his brother…huh!" Brad laughed.

"You know it! Are you eating tonight?"

"Something light…how about grilled cheese with some of mom's creamy tomato soup. I'll have a side of coleslaw with that and a piece of coconut cream pie." Brad placed his order like someone who knew exactly what he wanted.

"I'll bring you some cider to drink for now and then I'll be back with your dinner." Shawn said as he left.

"Shawn is an example of what Jesus can do to change a broken life. We're all praying that his brother will allow Jesus to change his life too." Brad offered an explanation to the girls.

Genie could feel a little warmth in her heart every time a new conversation happened that included God talk. The feeling that she wanted whatever it was that they had, was beginning to move inside of her. She was beginning to feel like there was something that she was missing. In the depths of her soul a stirring was starting. She would have to call it a desire. It was a new feeling for her.

Changing the subject, Brad asked, "So have you had a chance to see the hot spots of our little town today."

"We have seen some of it and it's lovely and quaint." Genie offered. "Some of the shops that are full of hand crafted items really caught our attention. We did a little shopping for items that we want to take back to the girls."

Brad caught the last sentence. "So are you getting ready to go back home?" There was a sinking in his stomach which again confused him. He knew this time would come. Why was he…what would you call this feeling…disappointed?

"You haven't talked with your mom yet have you?" Noelle asked.

"No. I had chores to do on the farm after class and I haven't seen her since I arrived." Brad wondered where she was going.

Noelle wasn't sure that it was her place to fill him in about the plans that the three women had made this morning. "Maybe we should wait for Angelina to talk to you. I don't want to step out of line."

"You can't leave me hanging like this. Do I have to go and get my mother?" Brad laughed.

"No. It's just…"

Brad could see that Noelle was uncomfortable so he said. "Why don't we enjoy our food? You can order some dessert and eat with me. I would love the company. Maybe later Mom will come and join us and we can talk then."

Noelle was instantly relieved. She knew that she was going to have to talk with Brad sooner than later. She just didn't want to have that conversation without Angelina having talked with him first. After all, she was a stranger moving into their home, even if it was temporary. She didn't know how Brad was going to feel about that.

So they ate and laughed. Brad was as easy to talk with as his mother was. They could both make you feel like they had known you for a lifetime. It made the evening pass quickly. Before they knew it Angelina was coming with a salad and a cup of tea to sit with them.

Being the no nonsense person that she was, she went right to the point. "Brad, I am glad that you stopped by. After talking this morning, we all decided that it would be best for Noelle to spend some time with us at the farm. I need another hand to replace Ally until she heals and Noelle needs a change of scenery. I think that God has just dropped her here to make my life easier. They are going back home early tomorrow morning to put a few things in order first. Then Noelle will be flying back out here. They have to leave the airport at 7:00 a.m. and I was thinking that you would have time to drop them off before heading to class. Does all of that work for you?"

Noelle watched for his reaction. She didn't want Brad to think that she was taking advantage of the kindness that his family had shown her. All she saw was a smile that was immediate. "That'll be great. It'll save you looking for someone. Seven in the morning works perfect. I have an 8:00 a.m. class which gives me plenty of time to get there." He turned to Noelle and asked, "How long will you be gone?"

"I have a return flight scheduled for the Monday after Christmas. But wouldn't it be better if I drove my car tomorrow and parked it at the airport? Then I wouldn't have to inconvenience someone to come back and pick me up. My flight doesn't get in until 10:00 p.m." Noelle wondered.

Brad answered instantly, "If you knew the area better, I would think that would be okay. You're so unfamiliar with these roads and it can be tricky especially in the dark of night. I would feel better if you would let me drive you. I really don't mind. It worked out perfectly. I won't miss class and I'll already be done with any work on the farm."

Noelle smiled, "Okay in that case, we would really appreciate it".

Angelina stood up, leaving half of her salad and said, "Good! Now that we have that all worked out, Noelle come with me and I'll introduce you to some of the staff that you'll be working with here." The two of them left.

"Brad I want to thank you for all of the kindness that you and your mother have shown to Noelle and me. I don't know what I would have done without you. I was frantic when I got home and Noelle was not there. You've both gone out of your way to help. I've never met anyone in my life that was so willing to change their lives to help someone in need." Genie reached across the table and squeezed Brad's hand.

"It was nothing. I'm sure that you would have done the same thing." Brad's response was so humble.

Genie answered immediately, "No Brad, I don't think that I would have been so quick to help. In fact I know that I wouldn't have gone out of my way to help a stranger unless it was on my terms. I haven't seen that in action well, ever. I assure you though now that I have been on the receiving end of that kind of response, I will be looking for ways to do so. We have lived a very blessed life and I'm beginning to realize that it's been a very selfish life. Noelle's mistakes, I believe, have come out of that. I didn't even see the brokenness in my own daughter let alone a complete stranger. That selfless giving comes so natural for your family. I've been blessed to meet you and your mother. I think that my family has so much to learn from you."

"Mrs. Smith don't try to learn it from our family. We're just humans and humans by nature fail. The only place that you will find faultless direction is in the Word of God. One of my favorite scriptures is ***Psalm 89:14-15 Righteousness and justice are the foundation of your throne; love and faithfulness go before You. Blessed are those who have learned to acclaim You, who walk in the light of Your presence, O LORD.*** As a young boy I learned that He is the light that marks my path. I found that I stumble less if I follow that light. It just seemed easier.

Genie was amazed at the wisdom that came from such a young man.

"I wish that I had looked closer. We didn't take the time to really find God. I didn't teach that to my girls. This has been a year of falling hard." Genie felt the heaviness pressing down on her for her failure.

"Well how lucky for you that we have a God who is just waiting to catch us when we fall. Our God is a God of love. He sent His Son to carry our burdens for us all the way to the cross. Jesus wasn't forced to go, He went willingly. No man put Him on the cross. In His brokenness, He climbed onto that cross all by Himself. He laid down His life so that all who call upon His name could have eternal life and there would be no separation from the Father. Mrs. Smith…He did that for you also. Have you ever called upon His name?" Brad asked with love.

Genie looked at the young man with tears in her eyes and said, "I think that I prayed a prayer like that years ago; but I don't think that it meant anything to me. I mean I think that I was just going through the motions. There really wasn't any change in my life."

Brad continued, "It isn't too late you know. He is always just waiting for us to come. I would love to pray with you right now if you would let me."

The tears slowly slipped from her eyes. "I would love you to do that."

Brad took those hands that were grasping for a life line and offered her the only thing that could make a difference. Forgetting the busyness of the restaurant, they bowed their heads and prayed.

"Father we are so thankful that You were willing to give the life of Your Son for wretched sinners like us. We acknowledge that we need a savior to save us from our sins and from the loneliness of a life spent without You. We know that only through the blood of Jesus can we live eternally with You. Thank you for the blood sacrifice of Your Son Jesus on that cross. We surrender our lives to You. We ask that You come into our hearts and be our Lord and Savior. We ask for the forgiveness of our sins accepting that Your blood has washed us white as snow. We acknowledge that we could never be worthy and that only by Your grace can we be free. We understand that as far as the east is from the west our sins have been removed, buried in the deepest sea never to be seen again. We believe that when You look at us You see us pure and sinless. And that we can rest assured knowing that we will spend eternity with You in Heaven. Father help us to rest in the assuredness of who You are so that we may walk in the blessings You have for us all the days of our life. And may our lives model You. In Jesus Name. Amen."

Genie prayed every word and knew that she was experiencing the love of the Lord. She knew that from this moment on her life would never be the same.

* * * *

Lying in bed that night, Genie was recalling all that had happened. Change…she wanted it more than she had ever wanted anything in her life. To understand what it means to live a life that is pleasing to God. She wanted that for each of her girls too.

Then forgive Genie. Forgive for my sake.

Those were the words that echoed over and over in her head as she lay down to sleep that night. She knew that they were from the Lord. She didn't understand all of it yet; but she had talked with Angelina before bed and was told that, "His sheep hear His voice." She was now a part of that fold and she never wanted to leave the protection of his arms again. She drifted off to sleep holding her daughter and talking to the Father. It had been a great day.

CHAPTER 23

PSALM 5:11-12
But let all who take refuge in You be glad;
let them ever sing for joy.
Spread Your protection over them,
That those who love Your name may rejoice in You.
For surely, O LORD, You bless the righteous;
You surround them with Your favor as with a shield.

RESTING IN HIS CARE

WAKING IN THE MORNING BROUGHT SUCH MIXED FEELINGS for both Genie and Noelle. By the end of this day Noelle would have once again faced the truth of her situation with her sisters. She would have to let them know that because of her choices, their lives again were about to change. There was sorrow in knowing that she was going to be the cause of more pain in their lives. But, her course was set; at least for the time being she had a plan. She would follow through to the best of her ability; being careful to listen for God's direction. Never again did she want to walk outside of his will for her life. She had learned the hard way that there are snares out there just waiting to capture you.

On the flip side, the excitement of knowing that her mom had also found a new life through Christ was filling her with joy. She wanted so much now to share what was happening with her sisters. Noelle wanted them to find the peace and contentment that she was learning only came through Christ.

If only…no…! She was not going to look back. She was looking forward step by step. The past was the past. She could not change it. She could, however, change the future. As a new creature, she could walk a life that was pleasing to the Lord allowing Him to direct her path. That was where she was headed.

Genie and Noelle left the room with their bags and entered into the wonderful smells of the kitchen. There sat Angelina and Brad with their heads bowed. They looked up and smiled.

"Good morning. We were just thanking God for His faithfulness. His mercies are new every morning. Come and have a good breakfast before you leave." Angelina motioned for them.

"Good morning to you. And He is faithful. Even when we don't know that we need Him to be. You've both taught us so much. I praise God for your willingness to be used by Him." Genie hugged Angelina before circling the bar and sitting down on one side of Brad as Noelle sat on the other side. Genie reached over and hugged Brad also.

Angelina slid a wrapped gift in front of Genie along with a plate filled with a cheese and veggie omelet, two strips of turkey bacon, rye toast, fruit and a cup of coffee that Genie had anxiously anticipated.

"What is this? We're the ones who should give you gifts for all that you've done for us." Genie said.

"After praying last night I didn't want you to go today without a weapon in your hand to battle the attacks that the enemy will throw your way." Angelina was definite about the gift.

Brad added, "Get ready. The enemy will come hard. He does not like it when his plan gets interrupted. He doesn't want anything good to happen to you. He certainly does not want you moving closer to God. Be ready. Fill up that God hole. We all have one; you know…the hole that only God can fill."

As she opened the Bible that they had given to her she said, "This is the perfect thing to fill that hole with don't you think…The Word of God! Thank you so much." Genie was thrilled.

As Angelina began to push a plate of the same amazing smelling food in front of Noelle, she was surprised when Noelle took the plate replacing it with a small box. At the same time Genie handed Brad a box that looked like his mom's only larger.

"You didn't have to do this." Brad said.

"And the two of you didn't have to be obedient to the Lord. I see people go through their whole life and never exhibit the love of the Lord. It's easy to be caught up in the world. Most of us don't even know that we should do things differently. But the two of you reached out to total strangers and our lives will be different because you were willing. We can't do enough to let you know how much we appreciate what you've done." Genie was starting to tear as she finished. "Now open them up." She smiled.

The girls were excited as they watched them open the gifts. They had found them in a small little shop in town yesterday and they were sure that they were perfect for the two who had impacted their lives in such a short period of time.

Angelina was the first to see what was inside. "Oh my… it's beautiful." In her hand she held a dainty cross of white gold. Draped across the top of the cross was a gold sash with the word servant etched onto it. Brad's was the same only a little bolder and on a leather cord instead of the tiny chair.

Genie and Noelle were so excited to see that the two who had become so important to them, seemed to like the gifts. They had looked for just the right something. Nothing seemed to say how much they appreciated this family; until they saw these.

"Jesus came as a servant. We've seen that quality in all that you do, not just here in your home; but, at the restaurant also." Genie was emotional trying to express how important these two people have become to her. She had been lost; but no more.

Angelina was shaking her head as the tears fell from her eyes. Yet, she smiled. There were no words to speak. Barely audible she said simply, "Thank you".

Taking a deep breath, she took out the necklace and began to fasten it on as she said, "Eat before your food is cold".

Brad turned on the stool so that his back was facing Noelle. "Will you do this for me?"

She took the cross out of the box, stretched it around his neck, and fastened it. "There you go!"

"Thank you Genie. It's nice. I'll wear it." He said as he faced her. Turning back to Noelle, he looked at her deeply and said, "Thank you Noelle". His smile filled her with an emotion that seemed to swell inside of her.

"You're welcome."

The girls chatted as they ate and began to make plans to leave. Brad was busy loading their bags into the SUV. He was taking his mom's vehicle and she would drive his truck to the restaurant today.

Angelina pulled Genie aside so that they could have a quick, private conversation. One that only mothers would understand. "I know how hard this is going to be on all of you. Please know that each and everyone of you are welcome at any time. Our home is plenty big enough to accommodate your whole family. I just wish it was closer." She drew Genie into a warm hug that said she understood what saying good-bye to her oldest daughter was going to cost her. Angelina was hoping to reassure Genie. She wanted her to know that she would make sure that Noelle was safe and taken care of. "It'll be okay. If you need to talk with me, I am always available. We will be in touch and if I ever think that you need to know something, I'll call you."

"I know. Even so, sending her back will be so difficult. And she's going to have so many decisions to make; hard decisions."

Angelina did know. "Remember that she's asking God to direct her path; a path that he already has set for her to walk down. He knew this day would come. He knows what is best and where she needs to go. He will not send her there by herself. He has a plan. He never leaves us alone. She won't have to walk that path by herself. God may put people in her life that will walk with her. Those people will never replace you. They'll just come along side of you." Angelina was so sure of what she was saying that it reassured Genie.

"You always know just what to say." Genie smiled.

"I read the book. It's full of answers. I'm really just stealing His words." Angelina laughed. One last hug and she said, "You better get going."

Genie headed to the front seat of the SUV and left Angelina to say good-bye to Noelle.

As Noelle exited the bathroom she walked straight to Angelina. She hugged her and then pulled back. "I've been wondering about Brad. Does he know?" She asked.

"He just knows that you came with some problems to work through. I did not feel that it was my place to tell your story. That's up to you to decide how much and when you want to discuss it. He understood." She nodded hoping to convey to the young woman that everything was okay.

"Okay. I guess that I'll talk with him when I get back. He certainly has the right to know. Thank you again. I'll see you soon." She turned to go and turning back added, "Thank you for my mom. I think that you've helped her get a new start on life. She needed that." And with a wave she was headed to the car and shortly they were pulling away from the house.

Father, bless their family today. Give them safe traveling and favor with Noelle's sisters as they talk with them tonight. Begin to prepare their hearts to respond with the type of love that only You understand. You are a God of mercy and your ways are not our ways. But, we are Yours and You know us better than we know us. Stretch forth Your hand and pour out on this family. Help them to love You more and more. AMEN.

CHAPTER 24

PSALM 34:4-8
I sought the LORD, and He answered me;
He delivered me from all of my fears.
Those who look to Him are radiant;
their faces are never covered with shame.
This poor man called, and the LORD heard Him;
He saved Him out of all His troubles.
The angel of the LORD encamps
around those who fear Him,
And He delivers them.
Taste and see that the LORD is good;
blessed is the man who takes refuge in Him.

CHANGING FROM PAST TO PEACE

SAYING GOOD-BYE TO ANGELINA AND BRAD HAD BEEN HARD. Even though they knew that they would see them again. There had been safety in their presence. Genie and Noelle were so new to this relationship with the Lord that neither one of them were sure that they would know how to create the atmosphere that they had just left. Yet they were sure of one thing…they wanted the peace that seemed to radiate in the lives and home of the Conroy family. Genie was sure that she would have many conversations with Angelina. She was also sure that the Bible that she had been given would become her favorite book. She was beginning to understand that it was more than a book; it was a road map for life. She intended to get on the right road and stay safely in the middle where she could not become entangled in the snares that would be set by the devil himself. She also planned to spend hours everyday in conversation with the Lord. She prayed as the plane brought her closer to her daughters at home.

Father, I don't know if I am doing this the right way so will You please help me. I want Your peace. I want to feel Your presence. I need You to guide and direct me and my girls. Father, You know better than any the wounds that have been created by Gale's leaving. To be honest with You, I don't know how to forgive him. I don't even know if I want to. I'm just hoping that You will help me forgive the way that You forgave. I know that as You hung on the cross You asked the Father to forgive the people who hurt You. Gale hurt me, and he hurt my...I mean our...girls. Help me to have a desire to forgive him; change my heart towards him. I'm guessing that it would be harder to be angry with someone that you pray for. So here goes...Father bless Gale and help him to find You. Help him to learn to walk in Your ways every day. Plus, Father could you give me a heart for the broken; teaching me to take my focus off of me and see through Your eyes. I want to love You more. And I want to love the way that You love. Thank you. AMEN

Noelle also was deep in thought as she watched the clouds pass by the window of the plane. Her mind was racing with the best way to tell her sisters about what was going on. Anaya would break for Noelle and would do everything in her power to try to understand. Nissa was her concern. Even though she had always been the peace maker in the family, she probably was the angriest with their dad. She seemed to feel the need to fix everything and keep the family as together as possible. Noelle wasn't sure how Nissa would react to all of this change. With Noelle moving to Indiana, their family was becoming even more fragmented. Nissa was not going to be very happy about that. Not that Noelle was pleased herself.

She would miss so much of the every day life of her sisters. They had always been each others biggest fans. You could always count on the family being in the crowd at your school activities. No one cheered louder than the sisters did. Now she wouldn't be there.

She could not think about those kinds of things now. She would not be able to get through this night if she did. She had to think about the words that she was about to say. But the harder she thought; the more nothing seemed to be right. She could feel the frustration building up inside of her. This was why she ran away. She did not want to have to tell them. Now here she was right back where she started. If she would have kept running she would not have had to …STOP RIGHT THERE. Noelle recognized these thoughts for what they were. These were just words being planted by satan himself to keep her in confusion. No…she wasn't going to dance with him any more. So she started to pray.

Thank you Father for letting me recognize the attack of the enemy. He is so subtle and he sneaks in so quietly that he can take back ground without a person even realizing it. Well…I say NO! I belong to You. You are going to direct my path. I will follow Your lead. I know that You will not take me anywhere that You do not equip me to go. Please surround me, Mom and my sisters with Your angels to keep our eyes focused on You and to keep the enemy outside. Father give me the words to speak to my sisters. Prepare them for what is about to come. Help them to understand; but, Father, mostly help this not to create more wounds. And help us to heal from the wounds that have already been created when Dad left. I don't know about forgiveness for Him. You'll have to walk me through that one. I've become kind of cold towards him. I guess that You want the best for him too. I just don't know how that fits in with how much pain we've all experienced since he left. I guess I don't have to understand it all at once.

I just want You to know that I'm willing to do what You want me to do. You're just going to have to help me do it. Thanks from me. Talk to You later. AMEN!

Noelle giggled to herself as she finished praying. To think that a God who created the whole world was only a whispered breath away was amazing in itself. It gave her a pretty powerful feeling to know that her best friend was God.

The plane was getting ready to land before Noelle and her mom even knew it. The time had literally flown by. They had both been so deep in thought that time had escaped them.

Genie reached over and took hold of Noelle's hand. "Here we go. It won't be long now. It's going to be okay. What is it that they say, 'All things are possible to those that love the Lord'. That's us Honey. We're not alone."

"Mom", Noelle began hesitantly. "Do you think that we could pray together?"

"I'm not very good at this; but, I think if we just tell Him what's in our hearts, He can make sense of our stumbling. Do you want to pray?"

"Okay…here goes!" Noelle said. Genie reached over and took her daughter's hand. "Father we need You to be with us tonight as we talk with the girls. Will You cause us to say the words that need to be said? And will You help them to understand and not be mad at me? I need them to love me Lord. And I need You to love me too. Thanks and AMEN. OH… OH…plus Lord if You could help us to teach them about You and the love that You have for them; it would be wonderful if our whole family could belong to You. Mom and I are agreeing on this. Thanks God. AMEN."

"Amen!" Genie smiled at the simplicity of the words spoken by her daughter to a BIG GOD! A God who is big enough to know what we need before we know it. She again thought about her gratitude for Angelina and all that they had learned.

It didn't take long to retrieve their car and start home. It would take less than an hour to get there. They decided to stop at the store and pick up food to make a nice family dinner. Their plan was to stay simple and have it ready when the girls were out of school.

They shopped fast and both of them were eager to walk into the home that had been their shelter in the storm. Home would always be home. But with what they had learned, they now realized that their protection from the storms of life doesn't come from walls that man builds; but from standing on the solid rock of Christ Jesus. There is a freedom that they were beginning to recognize. A life built on man's standards could come crumbling down. When we live to gain our acceptance from other people, we also have to accept when they judge us by their standards. They had experienced that first hand. But…a life built by the hand of God would stand the test of time. God's standards are based on the love that He has for us and His desire is only for our best.

****

Nissa and Anaya could smell Italian coming from the kitchen when they came home. It was immediately reassuring to know that life would look normal today. Mom was home and so was Noelle. They dropped their bags and headed towards the smell. As soon as they walked into the room, Noelle grabbed them and they hugged and danced around in a circle. Genie so enjoyed watching her girls looking so happy. Her heart did a quick jump as she thought; Will they be this happy by the end of the night?

"Come here and give me some of that love. Haven't I been missed too?" She said.

The girls wrapped her into their circle and for a brief moment life seemed complete. "Come on. Let's have dinner in here at the nook," Genie said. The breakfast nook seemed more quaint and intimate. As the girls started to eat, Genie said, "Maybe we should say a prayer over the food before we start." Silence fell over the group. The girls looked at Noelle and then at each other. This was the same family. But that wasn't the regular routine.

Before they could comment, Noelle said, "I think that's a great idea. Mom, do you want to pray?"

A little unsure Genie nodded and bowed her head giving time for the girls to do the same thing. Then she said, "Father God, thank you for the safe travel and for bringing us all together again. We are grateful. We ask that You will bless this food and the conversation that we share. In Your Son's name we pray. AMEN."

Well if that wasn't a show stopper Genie wasn't sure what was. It was almost comical the looks on Nissa and Anaya's faces. You could see that they thought something was terribly wrong. Praying wasn't something that happens around their house. Genie felt a twinge of guilt. "Lord forgive me for not teaching the importance of You to my family. I promise to do better now that I know." Genie quickly asked God for forgiveness.

My love does not come with condemnation. Love as You have been loved.

There was that voice that she could hear in her spirit. It always took her by surprise when she heard it. He was releasing her from those feelings of guilt and letting her know that it was going to be okay. Continue on. So she did. She began making small talk. Asking about the girls' day at school and making their meal as normal as usual. There would be time after to talk about serious things. But for now they would just enjoy each other's company.

After spaghetti with salad and homemade garlic bread, Noelle went to the freezer and brought out ice cream sundaes that she had made with mixed nuts, chocolate sauce, whipped cream, and a cherry on top. She thought about the home-made pies that they had eaten made by Angelina. This dessert wasn't nearly as amazing; but, it was made with love and wasn't that what really counts. Maybe someday she would learn to make pies.

As they ate their ice cream, Noelle knew that the time had come to talk with the girls about everything that had gone on. She started with, "I went on a journey that led me to the Lord. And in finding me, Mom also found the Lord. We accepted Him as our Savior and now we know that we're going to spend eternity with Him. We want you to know Him too. He'll make a difference in our lives. Without Him things can really get messed up and I know that first hand."

Anaya was the first to question, "What are you talking about?"

"Yah…I don't understand what all of this is about? You leave without telling anybody and then you say you're sorry; but, don't read the letter that I left. Next thing that we know Mom is flying off to some crazy place miles away so that you can explain everything to her. And now you have both found religion." Nissa was certainly not holding anything back.

Noelle started carefully, "I know that this doesn't make any sense right now. I'm going to explain so that hopefully it will. I just want you to know that the most important thing that came out of all of this is that we found a relationship with the Lord. You see, I made a mess of my life; but God came in and gathered up my mess and is helping me make it okay. Not the same; different; but, it is going to be okay." With that said, Noelle began to explain about feeling the need to leave to protect them. She told about purchasing the car, dropping out of school, and writing the note. She told them of the CD in the car and crying all the way that she drove. Then she told about the tire and Brad and his persistence. Noelle tried to describe what it was like meeting Angelina and the home where she had felt so welcome. She talked about their amazing relationship with the Lord and how they had shared that with Noelle and their mom. And then the question came…

Nissa asked, "What are you trying to protect us from?"

Noelle's breath caught in her throat. She felt like he air had been knocked right out of her. She closed her eyes and said, "Lord please give me strength…and be here with me. This is going to be so hard. I can't do this without You."

I am with you always.

Noelle felt His presence building her up. She opened her eyes and looked at each of the girls. "I'm pregnant."

Silence filled the air around them.

Anaya was instantly angry, "Who did this to you?"

Noelle could feel the anger as it began to build inside of Anaya. It was like watching a volcano about to erupt.

Anaya continued, "I know you and I know that you're not just sleeping around. You don't have a boyfriend. So I know that something happened. Tell me!"

Noelle couldn't tell anything but the truth. So she did. It wasn't easy and by the time that she was done talking, all four of them were crying.

These tears felt different. There was healing in these tears. Time went by as it sank in what Noelle was telling them. She was going to have a baby. The emotions began to roll through the girls; anger, pity, pain, regret, humiliation, revenge. You name it. But in the end, when all emotions had been voiced and discussed and calm was back; they began to talk.

Noelle explained that she left because she didn't want the girls to have to deal with the talk of the town again. She wanted them to understand that this wasn't their problem; that they had not caused it. She needed them to know that she didn't want it to affect them any more than it had to.

Nissa said, "That's great…but, this isn't your fault either. So the guy or guys do something like this over and over and they just keep getting away with it. Not fair!"

Genie spoke up for the first time. "It isn't fair. But this isn't the first time that we have learned that life isn't fair. Your sister has considered all possibilities and has made up her mind. She not only has carried the burden of what this could mean for you and me; but, she has given thought to what this would mean for a baby also."

She paused giving the girls time to absorb. Then continued with, "Would the baby carry a stigma knowing that he or she was conceived in a criminal act? If the news got wind of this through the court system it becomes a public record. Or would the baby be better off being raised by parents that want a child desperately. Noelle has to decide, does she keep the baby, or does she give the baby up for adoption."

"Noelle, what were you planning on doing about the baby when you left here?" Anaya asked.

Here I go Lord. Noelle prayed.

"When I left here I didn't care where I went I just wanted to get rid of this thing that had ruined my life. It wasn't until Angelina showed me through the Word of God that this baby is a living being, created by God with a purpose that He has already destined him or her for. I knew then that I could not abort the baby. That was when I began looking at this child as a precious life given to me by God. Not something that was forced on me by some sick guy that didn't know about God either."

She continued, "I'm trying to come to the point of actually forgiving the guy, whoever he is. That's what God wants me to do."

Noelle grabbed this moment to show them the God that she had found. "Finding God has given me a strength that I've never had before. I've now begun to understand that He had a plan for my life also. We can alter those plans by the choices that we make. I made choices to put myself into situations that opened me up to the attacks of satan. You see, what I had not taken into consideration is that satan and his demons are real and they are roaming this earth looking to really mess things up. I wish I had known what I know now. I would have made different choices. I would have stayed under the protective umbrella that God covers us with." Noelle took a moment to study the girls. They were very quiet. She wondered if they were getting any of this.

"I wish you could see the difference in Angelina and Brad's lives. There is such peace that radiates around them. It's so simple for them to just trust God. I want to live in that realm. I know that bad things can happen to good people. I'm learning that it isn't what happens; but, what you do with what happens. Right now, where I'm at, I'm choosing to trust God."

Anaya asked, "Are you telling us that you're okay with being pregnant and all of the changes that your life is going to take now? That it's alright with you that you're no longer in school? Or that you're going to either be a single mom or have a child somewhere that you aren't raising? Any of those options are crappy. And you are telling us that God will make them better. Is He a miracle worker?"

Noelle laughed and so did her mother. "Yes…as a matter of fact, He is a miracle worker. And part of the miracle that He's working in my life is that I'm working on forgiving Dad."

You would have thought that she dropped a bomb. Both of the girls exploded at the same time. They couldn't believe that she had said that. How could she actually think that he deserved their forgiveness? After all…they hadn't destroyed the family…he had. And they didn't want him to be forgiven.

Genie set back and for the first time she saw the brokenness in her girls. How had she missed it? Was she so caught up in her own pain that she could not see theirs?

. "Girls." The softly spoken words of their mother brought

their rampage to an end. "Noelle is right. Unforgiveness is only going to hurt us. Look at the bitterness that is building up inside of you. I hadn't even recognized it."

Genie continued, "Angelina said something that opened my eyes to it. She said that if he was not a selfish man, and we all know that your dad was a very giving man, then he must also be very broken knowing the pain that he's caused all of us. And the way that he set things up left him with no way to be forgiven. That means that he'll have to live with the guilt of what he did forever."

"I had to admit to myself that I had never given his feelings a thought through any of this grieving. I had only thought about you girls and myself. What about your dad? Think about it. This can't be easy for him. Regardless of what he did. The wondering must haunt him. So I have decided to begin to pray for him. I don't want to spend my life in anger. I think that you probably can't be angry with someone that you pray for on a regular basis."

Noelle smiled at her mom. She knew what a huge step toward healing this was for her. She couldn't help but thank God again for bringing Angelina into their lives. She was seeing God's hand at work here. Noelle wondered, would our family have ever healed if we hadn't met Angelina and her family; would we have found a Savior if I wasn't pregnant? Noelle could see the spark of fire that started in accepting that the baby was a blessing and that led them to the Lord. But the girls, where were they in all of this? Could they see the need for a Savior?

Lord, help my sisters to be able to sort through all that they have been given. I don't want to lose them. Find them right where they are at and don't let go of them. I know that You love them more than I can understand. Help me to show them You. We have such a short time together. Amen.

Noelle reached out to her sisters hoping to reach them right where they were at, “I was full of anger at Dad. This is where it got me.”

CHAPTER 25

PSALM 37:8-11
Refrain from anger and turn from wrath;
Do not fret—it leads only to evil.
For evil men will be cut off,
But those who hope in the Lord
will inherit the land
A little while, and the wicked will be no more;
though you look for them, they will not be found.
But the meek will inherit the land and enjoy great peace.

PRAYING FOR FORGIVENESS

As Genie lay in her bed, sleep was eluding her. She played over and over moments from the conversation with the girls. It bothered her that they were so bitter. She could feel the guilt begin to creep in. *Lord did I do this to them? Should I have been more aware of their vulnerability? I'm sure there were times that I let my anger at their dad spew out. I could have been much more cautious. Why didn't I realize what I was doing to them? I'm as much to blame as their dad is.* Genie was reeling from the realization that she could have caused the girls harm.

Love covers a multitude of sins. Forgive my daughter forgive. Forgive not only my son; forgive yourself.

She could feel the presence of her Savior. The peace began to seep through her slowly replacing the anxiety that was trying so hard to steal her sleep. Why had she waited so long to find the Lord? She had spent so many sleepless nights lost and lonely; too many nights where she had cried herself to sleep.

As she thought about Angelina, she remembered her new Bible. Getting up she crossed to the bag that sat waiting to be unpacked tomorrow. Unzipping it, she found the Bible that was calling to her like a new found friend. Taking it she crawled back into bed and tucking the covers around her, she split the leather bound cover and began to read where it opened in **The Book of John.** She read, In the beginning was the Word, and the Word was with God, and the Word was God. He was with God in the beginning. Through him all things were made; without Him nothing was made that has been made. In Him was life, and that life was the light of men. The light shines in the darkness, but the darkness has not understood it.

Genie pondered what she had just read. He was and is the light. What does light do? It makes the way clear. Without that light, you stumble around lost and searching. She thought about her life; where she and the girls were. The bitterness was building up in the girls and she realized that their lives could become full of darkness if the root of unforgiveness wasn't removed from their hearts.

Genie knew that Jesus was the only answer for the problem. So she prayed, *Father clear my girls of the root of unforgiveness. Help them to forgive their dad and to begin to heal. Lord give them the courage to face yet another struggle. But remind us that we are already conquerors through the blood that Jesus shed on the cross. Give me wisdom so that I can show the girls You. Help them to surrender and accept You as Lord. AMEN.*

Noelle was almost asleep when she heard her bedroom door open.

"Noelle…Noelle…" Nissa was calling.

"Noelle. Are you awake?" Anaya said.

"I am now." Noelle answered trying to pull herself back from the peaceful rest that she was just starting to reach. She wasn't upset that they had woke her up. In fact she welcomed the girls coming to talk with her.

"We couldn't sleep. Noelle we want to say that we are… well…

"What Nissa is trying to say is that we're sorry if we didn't understand where you are right now. This has all been so fast and crazy for us to grasp."

"Right; but we want you to know that we love you and no matter what you decide, we're on your side." Nissa finished with a big bounce on Noelle's bed; Anaya joining them.

The girls were full of questions about the pregnancy. They wanted to know how she felt. Was she scared? Had she been sick? They questioned her for the longest time? And then they said, "What do you think you're going to do?"

Noelle said, "I have no idea yet." She told them about Angelina and the restaurant. When she said that Angelina had opened her home and offered a job at the restaurant, the girls' hurt feelings came pouring out.

Anaya said, "How can you consider being so far away during a time like this? We want to be a part of what you are going through. Don't leave us out!"

"It's because of you girls that I need to go away. I know what this town is like. Let's not forget all of the talk when Dad left. I want to spare all of us from going down that road again. I hated that everywhere we went there were those pitying stares and the whispers behind the hands. I know that you felt the same way. We talked about it too many times, being made to feel like we had leprosy or something. It wasn't fair and we all hated it. Well, it will just happen all over again. Only this time it will be worse. I can hear it now. I will not put you through it. You will not have to suffer because of what I am going through.

"But this isn't your fault. Why do you have to pay the price? It makes me so mad when I think about what you went through." Anaya cried. "I want those boys to pay for what they did."

"I understand how you feel. And if there was a way that I could do something without my name being used, I would consider that. But without a huge court battle, I can't see that happening. You know DNA and all of that. The truth is, I couldn't tell them who the guy was. I had never seen him before. I would come closer to identifying the guy who gave me the drink. Everything that happened later is gone from me. I don't remember anything until the next morning when I woke up groggy. That was really the only time that I saw him and his back was to me. At that point, I was just trying to get out before anyone saw me. I was so ashamed. I didn't want to be associated with those people ever again."

The girls wrapped their arms around me and held me close. We all cried.

After a few minutes of soaking in their love, Noelle felt the nudging of the Lord and decided to grab the opportunity. "Listen to me. If I hadn't put myself in that situation, I couldn't have been hurt. It seemed harmless at the time. There was never a thought or an inclination that I was in danger. Do you understand what I am saying; you have to avoid those places. You have to know that danger can be where you least expect it. Never let your guard down. All you have to do is open the door a little bit and satan sneaks right in. But, if you keep the door closed and guarded, he cannot harm you. Do you get that?" Noelle finished.

"Do you really believe all of that devil stuff?" Anaya asked.

"I know that this is all new to us. But I have to believe that if there is good; then there is evil. I have seen the 'Hand of God' at work in my life these past few days. I watched as

He guided and directed me to a safe place. He took care of me and dropped me into a spot where I could be ministered to by someone who understood where I was. There is so much more that happened in the conversations and the kindness that was shown to me and then to Mom. It didn't have to be that way. God was preparing me even in the music on the CD that was the only thing that I could listen to in the car. I had no idea where I was going. I was just driving. I could have gone anywhere; but He took me to a house where they would show me what He looks like. And then showing me wasn't enough. They were obedient to offer me the Lord. And then Mom came and she saw what they had and what we were missing. I wish that you could have experienced what we saw. Their life with God is so much better than our life without. I want us to have more. That more comes with acknowledging Him as out Lord and Savior. It comes with understanding that we need to be saved. We can't do it alone. It's too hard. When I accepted Him everything fell into place. I don't have all of the answers; but I know that I have Him and with that knowledge comes a reassurance. I know that He'll direct my path so that I don't make any more mistakes. He wants that personal relationship with me. He protected me from myself even when I didn't love Him. He loved me first. I want you to find what I've found." Noelle said.

Nissa asked, "Is it as simple as asking Him to do that? You know what I mean, asking Him to be Savior of my life?"

"It is that simple. He won't push His way in. But He's just waiting for us to ask Him in."

"If we wanted to do that tonight, what would we do?" Anaya questioned.

"We would pray. I don't know all the right words to say. But I understand that He hears from our hearts. He knows what our hearts are saying. I don't think that it matter if we don't say beautiful prayers. I think that He just wants us to say sincere prayers. He wants to know that we love Him."

Noelle cautiously asked, not wanting to push the girls into anything that they didn't really mean, "Are you saying that you would like to say a prayer asking God to come into your hearts?"

Nissa said, "It's so hard being so angry at Dad. It colors every thought that I have. I can see where it's making me bitter. The relationships with my friends are different. I don't like the person that I'm becoming. If God can make my life different, then I'd like to find out who He is."

"I hear you talk about Him like He's right beside you. I don't understand how that can be. How do you talk with him as if He is right with you? How can He answer you?" Anaya was puzzled.

"I don't have all of the answers. This is all new to me too. I guess that when you ask Him into your heart, He sends the Holy Spirit to live in you. When He answers my questions, or just lets me know He's there, I feel it. I can hear His direction without really hearing it. Angelina said that as we study His Word, it is buried in our hearts. Then when we need direction, He brings it to our remembrance. All I know is that He loves me and I need Him to love me."

"Noelle could I pray right now?" Anaya asked.

"Me too? I want Him to love me too." Nissa said.

My heart was flowing over with gladness. I can't even explain what I was feeling. This was answered prayer. Mom and I had asked God to bring the girls to Him and here they were. I was bubbling.

I hugged them and said, "Okay let's pray together. You just repeat everything that I say." Noelle bowed her head and clasped her hands together. The girls followed her.

"Father God, thank you for sending Your Son, Jesus, to the cross. We acknowledge that we are lost and that we are going to hell without His blood that was shed on that cross. We ask that You come into our hearts and forgive our sins. We know that we are sinners and without You we have nothing. Please be our Savior. We give You our lives. We love You Jesus. AMEN."

The girls were all hugging, yelling, and jumping on the bed when Genie threw open the door and said, "My goodness what is going on? What's up with the three of you?"

Nissa said, "Anaya and I prayed with Noelle and we asked Jesus into our hearts".

"It's true. We're a family of believers Mom!" Anaya said.

Genie looked at Noelle who was smiling from ear to ear.

"It's true Mom." Noelle answered nodding her head.

"Praise God! Praise God!" The next thing we knew Mom was up on the bed and all of us were jumping and dancing together. It was a night to celebrate. The sheep had all come home.

CHAPTER 26

PSALM 30:1-5
I will exalt You, O LORD,
for You lifted me out of the depths
and did not let my enemies gloat over me.
O LORD my God, I called to You for help
and You healed me
O LORD, You brought me up from the grave;
You spared me from going down into the pit.
Sing to the LORD, you saints of His;
praise His holy name.
For His anger lasts only a moment,
but His favor lasts a lifetime;
weeping may remain for a night,
but rejoicing comes in the morning.

THANKFUL FOR ANSWERED PRAYER

THE NEXT FEW DAYS IN THE SMITH HOUSE WERE FULL OF excitement and activity. This week was Christmas and there was a tree to get and decorate, special food to prepare, and gifts to buy and wrap.

Underlying all of the joy of the season was the knowledge that Noelle was going to fly back to Indiana in a week. She was going to start a new life and for the first time the girls were going to be separated. It had been a tough decision. Nissa and Anaya were adamantly opposed to the distance that would be between them. It was Genie, though she wasn't any happier about the choices, that helped them to agree. She reminded them that this decision was not really theirs to make.

She said, “Noelle is the one who is going to have to live with the consequences to the decisions that are made from this point on. I feel like we need to support her in whatever she thinks is best.”

Begrudgingly the girls agreed that they would do what Noelle thought was best. But…not without complaining about how much they were going to miss her. They wanted to share in her pregnancy.

Noelle was convinced that it was best for her mom and sisters if she wasn’t around town.

They all agreed that they would keep this a secret and the only person that they would tell would be Aunt Debbie. She was too much a part of their family not be involved. Genie volunteered to talk with her sister.

So all of that being decided, they agreed to enjoy the week. And that is exactly what they did. They laughed. They baked. They ate. And on Sunday they went to church together. Genie’s heart swelled as they began to read the Bible and pray as a family. There was an excitement in their home that had never been before. At the end of their prayers they always asked God to heal their broken hearts and they asked that He would bless their dad wherever he was. Nissa and Anaya wasn’t sure about praying for their dad yet; but, they surrendered to the idea allowing that it would help them to feel better. However, they had admitted that as they were obedient to pray, God was softening their hearts to the idea.

It was a good week and Christmas morning was full of laughing. They had a wonderful breakfast and then leisurely sat and opened presents. The best gift of all was a surprise for Noelle. It was a scrap booking album for the baby. The girls had taken pictures of Noelle and began to write a story about a beautiful girl who chose the gift of life for her child. They had written a wonderful story leaving spaces to fill in pictures as the pregnancy progressed. Noelle looked at the girls.

Nissa said, "We know that you haven't decided whether to keep the baby or put him or her up for adoption yet. But either way, this baby needs to know about the person who chose life in a complicated situation. This baby needs to know that he or she was loved." Noelle started to tear and all that she could voice was an emotional, "Thank you. It's a beautiful idea."

The week came to an end all too quickly and the packing began. She chose her clothes carefully. She was not sure how long she would be able to wear her own clothes. She picked items that were loose fitting and stretchy. The day before she left they went shopping and bought a few nice pairs of black pants that were a relaxed fit and a few blousy tops. She remembered seeing that the workers at the restaurant were all wearing black pants and white shirts. She made sure that she was set to go. She wanted Angelina to know that she was ready to work. She was not there to sponge off of anybody. Noelle intended to pull her own weight.

The day came and she was all packed; they all agreed they just wanted to stay home and spend the day together. They watched a movie, nibbled on light meals, and spent a lot of time talking. It was decided that when the girls got to spring break, Noelle would fly home. Three months…that was all that they had to be apart. The time would go fast. The girls were playing basketball. Genie agreed to tape all of their games so that they could send the DVDs to Noelle. She was sad that she wasn't going to be there. Noelle promised to take lots of pictures as her belly grew. Of course they would talk everyday on the phone. They even changed phones. For Christmas, Genie had bought all of the girls iPhones. They could take pictures and send them back and forth. It would feel more as if they were more connected. Noelle was going to take the laptop with her. That way they could Facebook back and forth too.

The time came to leave. They packed the car and headed

to the airport.

"No tears!" Noelle said as she prepared to board the plane.

"Three months that's all we have to do…just three months." Anaya said.

Nissa chimed in with, "The time is going to go fast. You'll see."

Noelle hugged each of the girls and then looked at her mother. Genie's eyes became fluid. "I know! I am trying. Give me a hug. We are only a plane jump away if you need us."

Genie grabbed a hold of her oldest daughter and squeezed her as tight as she could. "I love you!" She whispered into her ear.

"I know Mom…thanks for everything. We're going to be okay…right?"

"Right." Genie nodded. Turning her daughter she sent her off towards the plane and as soon as she was out of sight the three girls sat down in the closest chairs and started to cry.

Noelle was wiping her eyes as she boarded the plane that would take her away from those that loved her at a time when she needed them the most.

The Lord could hear the prayers of all four.

When Noelle's plane left, she was two months pregnant. He due date was July 31. Seven months to make the most important decisions that she would ever make.

* * * *

Brad's day had dragged on forever. Today Noelle was flying back in. He was going to pick her up at the airport at 10:00 p.m. He had checked several times to make sure that everything was on time and he knew there were no delays. His mom and Genie had talked while Noelle was home. He even knew that his mom and Noelle had talked. He had no communication with Noelle while she was gone. There was certainly an excitement brewing inside of him. Try as hard as he could to remain calm, he had to admit, at least to himself, he couldn't wait. Today he would see the little woman child again. He had thought about her more times than he wanted to acknowledge while she was gone. She had a way of creeping into his daily thoughts at times when he least expected it. He reminded himself often that this was someone with a huge problem. So he prayed, God if this is a bad idea to become caught up in her life, then please protect me from that. But the thoughts still came. Brad had never had, or really wanted a serious relationship in the past. Life was full enough; and complicated. He had school, the farm, and the restaurant. Then there was always something to help his mom do. The days came and the days went. Life just kept rolling on; until that morning when he saw that car. And nothing had been the same for him since. He thought about her. Wondered what she was doing and looked forward to this day when she would return to the farm. Now the day was here. He couldn't wait to get to the airport. In fact he was there over an hour early. He told himself it was just in case the plane was early. But…he knew the plane was on time! He had checked…often.

Brad sat in a chair facing the big windows that allowed you to see the planes coming in. He checked his watch and he studied the monitors that kept him updated on the flights. He began to pass the time by praying. *God, Noelle is flying back into my life and I can't explain this feeling. I don't even know this woman; yet, I am so excited that I can't hardly stand the wait. Is this feeling from You? Are You placing this woman in my life as a mate? I've been faithful to remain pure waiting for the day when You would give me the woman that You have created just for me. Lord protect my heart. If this isn't of You, then I ask that You shut these feelings off. But, if this is You, then prepare Noelle's heart for a relationship with me. God, if You are going to join us together as man and wife; bless all the days of our life together.*

Love as I have loved you.

Brad knew the voice that had just answered his prayers. He knew that God had just given him the go ahead to pursue a relationship with Noelle. What he didn't know was what did that relationship look like. At what point was he going to find out her secrets. He didn't have those answers. What he did know, was that God wasn't going to bring him to this point without equipping him with the tools to finish walking down the path. What he now was certain about was that the woman coming off the runway terminal at any moment was going to be his wife and that together they would build a life.

* * * *

Noelle had slept on the flight to Indianapolis. She woke as the stewardess tapped her shoulder and said, "Time to prepare to land". Noelle put her tray back in the upright position and made sure that her seat belt was fastened. The landing was smooth and she was exiting in no time at all.

There had been no time for Noelle to think about Brad until she boarded the plane. Her life had been so full of her family that she hadn't looked into the future. As the plane brought her closer to Angelina and Brad, she had to admit that there was a certain amount of excitement in seeing them again. She didn't think that it all had to do with Angelina. Though Brad and her had not had much time together after he had rescued her, there was always a special feeling that filled her when he was around; or even when she thought about him. She didn't even know how to describe it; bubbly, maybe would be a good word. She chuckled to herself as she thought that.

Then she would remember her situation. The reality was that no one as special as Brad Conroy was going to want to get caught up in her mess. He didn't even know about the baby. She knew that was something that she would have to fix right away. If she was going to be living in his home, he certainly had the right to know the truth. Then that would be that. Brad Conroy was the kind of man who could have the best that God had. She wasn't that person any more. She had always planned that she would go to her marriage bed pure. Well…that's one of the consequences that she was going to have to live with. And so was the man that she would eventually marry. Brad didn't have to settle. She could tell from the way that he treated his mother that he understood God's desire to honor one another. No…Brad would always be the gentleman. But as far as a relationship with her, that would be beyond what God called him to do. So Noelle went to sleep accepting that they would just be friends.

* * * *

Brad spotted her before she saw him. His heart began to beat fast. She had that groggy little girl look. Like she had been sleeping. Her hair was curling softly around her face; with a little bounce as she walked down the runway. He wanted to run up and sweep her into his arms. But he wouldn't. He would be patient and wait on God. He enjoyed that she was looking for him. It made him feel special.

He headed towards her and waved. She saw him. He was done the very minute that she smiled that huge smile that said she was excited to see him.

He put his arm around her shoulders and gave a soft squeeze. He said, as he took her carry on bag from her, "Hey little one!"

She looked into his eyes and with that killer smile said, "Hey to you".

"Was your flight okay?"

"It must have been. I slept through the whole trip." She answered back.

"Great! Then you should be rested enough to stop and get

some supper. I haven't eaten yet. I'm starved." Brad continued, "Let's get your bags and get out of here. We'll call Mom and let her know that you're here safe and that we're going to get something to eat."

"Sounds good to me."

He took her hand and led her to the luggage pickup. She loved the feel of her hand in his. Yet, she cautioned herself not to get attached. She didn't need her heart broke in the complication of her life as it is. Besides, he was just helping her. Don't read anything into this. She warned herself.

Brad hung on to her hand as they maneuvered through the human traffic of the airport. He would have been content to walk for hours as long as he could continue to hold her dainty hand. He noticed how nicely it fit in his big farm hands. He could close her hand completely into his palm. Her hands were so soft. He wondered what she was thinking about his hands. They were the hands of a working man; rough from farm work. He hoped that they would convey that these were hands that would protect her regardless of what they faced. Yet as he held on gently, he hoped that she realized they were hands that would lovingly hold a baby as her daddy rocked her off to sleep.

With the luggage gathered and tucked into the back of the SUV, Brad maneuvered the crazy airport traffic. He said, "Must be a lot of people in need of being somewhere else tonight".

She smiled. "Thank you for picking me up. You were right. I would have been lost in no time. This is so confusing with all of the traffic and lights."

"It was my pleasure. I have to be honest with you. I've been really excited to see you again. In fact…I think I really missed you." He looked at her hoping to see what kind of reaction that statement brought. It was too dark and he couldn't read her face.

Noelle was surprised by what he said. She didn't know how to reply. She sat quiet for a moment and then decided that it wasn't fair for her to let him think she was someone that she wasn't. So she said, "Brad, I think that we need to talk. There are some things that I need to share with you. We didn't get the opportunity to talk much when I was here before. I want you to know what is going on in my life now that I'm here to stay for a while."

"Okay. Can it wait until we get to the restaurant? I want to be able to focus on what you're saying."

"Absolutely."

From that point on the ride was quiet. Noelle wasn't sure what Brad was thinking.

Brad on the other hand was praying, *God, I don't believe that I heard Your voice wrong. I asked You to protect my heart. I'm just going to trust You. Lead me where You want me to go. Make sure that I don't get out ahead of You. I'm following Your lead. AMEN.*

Love as I have loved you Brad. Love as I have loved you.

"Okay Father. I got it."

"Do you like Mexican?" Brad asked her.

Noelle answered quickly, "I do. I love Mexican."

"Great! Right up here there is a family owned Mexican restaurant. The owners are the nicest people. I try to stop here any time that I have to come into Indianapolis. We'll eat there. There are some private tables in the back where we can have a quiet conversation. How's that?"

Noelle smiled, "It sounds wonderful. Thank you."

As they entered the restaurant Noelle knew Brad was right. The place was beautifully decorated and the smell was mouth watering. They were given the back table which was right across from a lighted fireplace. The atmosphere was quiet and romantic. Noelle wasn't sure that she would have chosen something so intimate for this conversation.

"Would it be okay if I ordered for us? I'd love for you to sample some of my favorite dishes."

"Oh that would be fine. I like everything, spicy or not. Surprise me." She said.

Noelle excused herself while Brad was ordering and when she came back there was an icy drink in front of her.

She sat down and he nodded at the glass. She gave him a quizzical look, as she smelled the rich aroma of the drink. Smiling she carefully sipped. "Wow! This is wonderful. What is it?"

"It's Horchatta. It's a rice and cinnamon flavored drink. If we're going to have a serious conversation, there's enough sugar in it to keep you up all night." He smiled.

The waiter brought a big platter of all kinds of different appetizers and a second bowl of homemade chips with salsa. The food looked amazing. She couldn't wait to taste it.

"I hope this is all we're eating. I can't imagine having room for a meal after this." She said.

"Oh no! We're just getting started. Their wet burritos are the best I've ever had. I hope you like a lot of cheese."

Noelle laughed, "I'm going to need a doggy box".

He smiled, "So…let's talk. You tell me whatever you feel like you need to. I am a great listener. I just sometimes need some processing time. I don't like to respond until I know that I understand. So if I'm quiet and don't comment, don't read into it, I'm just listening and thinking."

Brad made Noelle feel very comfortable and safe. So she began at the beginning. That seemed like the only place to start so that he would understand. She told about her dad and their life before and their life after. She talked about her brokenness. How she began to make poor choices out of her wounds and the danger that came due to putting herself in the wrong place.

Then she told of the consequence that she is now going to

live with. She explained that when he found her that morning, she was working through a plan to remove the problem.

"You see", Noelle sighed, "it was God's intervention that brought me to your family. I didn't even know that He would direct my life; and yet, He did. He saved this baby through you and your mom."

Noelle stopped talking after what seemed like forever. She wondered what he was thinking.

"I'm not the kind of girl that 'sleeps around' is how my sister put it. I had intended to go to my husband pure. I don't know who the guy was that stole that from me. I just woke up that morning and had no idea what had happened. The last thing that I remember, some guy was getting me a drink."

"Don't get me wrong. I blame no one but myself. I shouldn't have been at that sorority party. This is my problem to work through. A positive pregnancy test, what should have been one of the most exciting times of my life; became the worst life-changing moment." Noelle stopped and taking a deep breath she asked, "Are you processing? Or are you in shock?"

"He nodded at her and asked, "Could we pray?"

"Okay."

Brad reached over and took her hands in his. Without taking his eyes off of her eyes, he slowly raised her hands up to his lips and gently kissed them. Then bowing his head he said…

"Father God with You there are no mistakes. You knew this baby before he or she was formed. And You have a purpose for this life. Heal the wounds that have been inflicted onto Your daughter. Help her to see that when she repented You now see her white as snow. Let her see herself as You see her. There is no place for condemnation in Your kingdom. Help us all to remember that we live under the laws of grace and mercy. Not one of us is worthy without being covered by

Your Son's blood. We rest in your hands. We ask that You hold us close and never let us go. Father, I ask that You bind Noelle and myself together with a cord of three. You have brought us into each other's lives and with Your help we will remain together forever. With You intertwined with us, nothing is impossible. We thank you God for blessing our lives. We ask Your protection on this baby and on this pregnancy. We rest in Your care and we love You. AMEN."

Brad opened his eyes as Noelle slowly raised her head. She was looking into the most loving eyes that she had ever seen. She felt like she could see into the depths of him. There were tears rolling down her cheeks.

He slowly raised his hand to wipe the tears from her face. "It's okay." Was all that Brad could say.

"You don't understand." Noelle said.

"No, I think that I do. God was at work in this from the very beginning. What I didn't understand was the crazy immediate attachment that I felt to you. From the very beginning I knew that you were different. I've never been in a serious relationship. I've just been waiting for God to bring the person that He had made just for me. That's why I couldn't understand the feelings that I experienced every time that I was around you; or every time that I thought about you."

Brad continued, "While I was waiting for you to arrive tonight, I began asking God about all of this, and He said, 'Love as I have loved you'".

"I asked Him a second time in the SUV when you told me that we needed to talk. He told me the same thing, 'Love as I have loved you'".

"You can call me crazy; but I think that you're going to find out that God directed this so that we would be together. I think that I have loved you from the moment that I met you. And if God is allowed to have His way, you're going to love me too."

"Oh Brad! I don't know what to say?"

"You don't have to say anything. We aren't under the gun. We'll take our time and see if you develop feelings for me."

"However" he said with a smirk, "do you know that the Bible doesn't say that a wife has to love her husband? It says that she has to respect him. A husband is called to love his wife as Christ loved the church. I already love you."

"I didn't know that. I want to love the man who becomes my husband. But if respect is the first step, then that was easy. I respect you now. And I know that whoever you marry will be the luckiest woman in the world."

He smiled and winked at her saying, "Then don't let that guy get away".

THOUGHTS FROM THE AUTHOR

I APOLOGIZE FOR LEAVING YOU HANGING AT THE END OF THE book. I know that you must have all kinds of questions. Where is Brad and Noelle's relationship going? Will they become a couple? Will Noelle fall deeply in love with Brad? What about the baby? Will Noelle keep the baby? Will she give the baby up for adoption?

I promise to answer all of those questions in the sequel, **"Love Abounds"**. Watch and see if Brad and Noelle are obedient to God's direction and see what plan God, in all of His majesty, masterminds for them, and their families.

I do not want you to lose focus of what the purpose of this book is though. Do you know that over 4000 babies are aborted every day in America? Since 1973 we have murdered over 45 million babies. We have abolished one whole generation of people. They say that the mother's womb has become a tomb.

To those of you who have had abortions you must know that it is a sin. But it is not an unpardonable sin. Run to the mercy seat of the Lord. Ask God to forgive you.

> ***I John 1:9*** *If we confess our sins, He is faithful and just and will forgive us our sins and purify us from all unrighteousness.*
>
> ***Ephesians 1:7-8*** *In Him we have redemption through His blood, the forgiveness of sins, in accordance with the riches of God's grace that He lavished on us with all wisdom and understanding.*

If you are considering an abortion, don't make a decision that you will regret forever. Abortion does not solve problems. It creates them. It can cause emotional problems through grief and guilt. It is a painful, physical experience. There can be so many physical complications. The feeling of emptiness can last a lifetime. A parent is forever, even if the child has died. Abortion is the choice of a frightened woman. As a society we are called to reach out in love with help. Jesus ushered in grace and truth.

God holds us to a higher standard. Life begins at conception. All life has value, young and old. Don't be led astray. Call abortion what it is—murder. When the baby is called just a fetus, know that fetus is the Latin word for child. A fetus is not just a "mass of cells" or a "cluster of cells". It is more than the "product of conception". It is life with a purpose. At the moment of conception God breathes the breath of life into that baby. From that moment on, it has a spirit that is in the image of God. That spirit has a life in eternity. For God knows the plans that He has for that child; plans to prosper him or her and give peace. A life is no accident. It is a divine appointment. God can take the mess that we make of our lives and make it a creation of beauty. He loves us all that much. He had enough love for us to give His own Son, Jesus, as a ransom for our lives. Don't let the devil win. Be strong. You serve a mighty God. Give Him the opportunity to love you.

If you haven't asked the Lord Jesus Christ into your heart to be your Lord and Savior and you would love to feel the joy that only comes from knowing Him and living within His protection, I would love the opportunity to pray with you.

Right now…right where you are…repeat this pray with me.

Lord Jesus, I come to You today wanting to know that I am forgiven for the sins that I have committed. I want to be Your child an heir to Your eternal kingdom. Cleanse

me from my sins and see me white as snow. Help me to be a new creation, loved by You. The old is passed away and the new has begun. I am now Your child never to be separated from You again. By praying this prayer I have sealed my place in Heaven forever to live with You. Thank you for forgiving me and for loving me as Your own. In Jesus' Name. Amen

God loves you…

Be CAPTURED!

Brenda, Angel Wing Ministries

These books continue to be an obedience to serve God. It is still my desire that whoever reads these words will find a burning passion to know my Savior more.

I would love to hear from you.

Comments or questions can be directed to Facebook at Angel Wing Ministries. We also are working on a web page at www.angelwingministries.com

Watch for the sequel
"LOVE ABOUNDS"
Coming in the soon.

PROVERBS 16:3
Commit to the Lord whatever you do;
And your plans will succeed.

God Bless,
Brenda Conley

Made in the USA
San Bernardino, CA
01 December 2012